Blue-Blooded Romeo

(book six of the Royal Romeos series)
by Jenny Gardiner

What people are saying about Jenny Gardiner's books:

"A fun, sassy read! A cross between Erma Bombeck and Candace Bushnell, reading Jenny Gardiner is like sinking your teeth into a chocolate cupcake...you just want more."

--Meg Cabot, NY Times bestselling author of Princess Diaries, Queen of Babble and more, on Sleeping with Ward Cleaver

"With a strong yet delightfully vulnerable voice, food critic Abbie Jennings embarks on a soulful journey where her love for banana cream pie and disdain for ill-fitting Spanx clash in hilarious and heartbreaking ways. As her body balloons and her personal life crumbles, Abbie must face the pain and secret fears she's held inside for far too long. I cheered for her the entire way."

--Beth Hoffman, NY Times bestselling author of *Saving CeeCee Honeycutt* on *Slim to None*

"Jenny Gardiner has done it again--this fun, fast-paced book is a great summer read."

--Sarah Pekkanen, NY Times bestselling author of *The Opposite of Me*, on *Slim to None*

"As Sweet as a song and sharp as a beak, *Bite Me* really soars as a memoir about family--children and husbands, feathers and fur--and our capacity to keep loving though life may occasionally bite."

--Wade Rouse, bestselling author of At Least in the City Someone Would Hear Me Scream

Chapter One

THERE were times in her life when Stella Whitaker wished she could drop all pretenses of civility and speak her mind, and now was decidedly one of them. She'd spent the last several days with minimal sleep, working late into the night to complete her first commissioned wedding cake for a bride getting married in Florence, Italy. After training in pastry for half a year at the elite French school of culinary arts, l'école Marondi, this was her first freelance hire, and she'd felt enormous pressure to succeed wildly with this project. It had the potential to lead to more such jobs. The cake turned out exceptionally well, the bride was elated, and now she and her friend Alexa Hanigan, who'd helped transport the masterpiece, were in line to board their flight back to Paris, where they would both begin their final class at Marondi. Yet out of nowhere, the rudest man accosted Stella.

"*Scusi, signora.*" At first, she thought maybe he was trying to make small talk, maybe coming on to her. He was a handsome man: tall, with a broad chest that narrowed down to slim hips, highlighted by—let's face it, it was impossible not to notice—a well-endowed bit of window dressing. She was starting to think she could find plenty of ways to have a little fun with a guy like that. Until he pointed at her boarding pass and ruined that fleeting fantasy. "I'm afraid you're in the wrong line."

Stella squinted at him, wondering what business it was of his what line she was in, although she was in the right one anyhow. As she looked at him, she noticed he had the warmest brown eyes, with thick, long lashes that were, to be truthful, wasted on a guy. Though they looked damned good on him.

"Pardon?" she said, wanting to get the ninety-minute flight from Milan to Paris over with so she could get some shut-eye.

He pointed again at her boarding pass. "*Ecco*. Here. Your boarding pass has you in '*zona quattro*,' zone four, but you're standing in the group for zone two. I'm afraid you need to go to the end of that line." He pointed to a queue that had a good thirty people in it. She counted the number of people in front of her in the current line in which she stood: only about six. She furrowed her brow. Who was this clown, trying to police the airport line? So maybe she hadn't looked at her boarding zone and instead simply followed Alexa without thinking. What was the harm to him?

"Look, uh, *signor*," she said with emphasis, "my friend is in zone two and we're sitting together so I got in line with her, assuming we'd be boarding at the same time. See, look at her boarding pass." She pulled the slip of paper from her friend's hand and held it up next to hers. "See, she's in seat 27A and I'm in… I'm in…"

"Ah… It appears that was the confusion," he said. "You're in seat 14D."

Stella shook her head, her long, auburn waves dancing angrily across her shoulders. "Wait a minute. That's not right. We're supposed to be seated next to each other. What the—"

She was about to stomp over to the gate agent to fix the situation when an announcement was made that the flight was overbooked and the airline needed volunteers to change flights, which meant there would be no correcting of wrong seating assignments. Stella groaned. She still didn't understand why the guy had to be such a bossypants about it. Who died and made him the head of airport security?

Nuisance Man nodded to the bags Stella was hauling. "You know you're only allowed one carry-on item."

She glared at him. "Of course. And I have one carry-on item."

He then pointed to her shoulders, one of which held a purse, the other a computer bag. "They're not going to let you on with both of those."

She frowned. "They're my personal items."

He pursed his lips and shook his head, which made Stella more crazy. The old "silent-but-I'm-right" treatment. How on earth had she ever found herself in a weird little queue war with this complete stranger?

But he was on to other topics of discussion.

"What a coincidence—it looks like your friend and I are seated next to one another." The man combed his fingers through his thick, wavy dark hair. As much as Stella wanted to hate him for being such a buzzkill, he was awfully easy on the eyes. Even her overly tired, void-of-a-good-night's-sleep green eyes. She smiled one of those smiles you'd force onto your unhappy face after the nurse tells you you've gained ten pounds at your annual physical. *Woo-hoo*. Mr. Tall, Dark, and Rigid gets to sit next to her friend and she's stuck in *zona quattro*, waiting forever to get on the plane. Grrrr.

The man reached his hand out to Alexa. "Forgive my manners. I'm Domenico. Domenico Romeo." He turned and nodded as well to Stella and attempted to shake her hand, which she ignored and instead crossed her arms and tucked said hands neatly beneath her armpits. *Zona quattro my ass.* Those airline zones were bogus, anyway. Every time she flew, she got stuck in the one that was the last to board. It didn't matter where she sat on the plane, it was always the wrong damned zone. All she wanted was to get on the plane, put her seatbelt on, and have the plane take off so she could finally settle in for a cat nap, which would have to suffice until she returned to her apartment.

Ugh, but the Nudge seemed to want to engage in conversation for some reason, which was plucking her last nerve.

"Yeah I had hoped to get a seat in first class or at least business class, but I had to change flights at the last minute, and this was all they had."

Stella turned so that only Alexa could see her and pretended to be him talking, taking great joy in mocking him. Pretentious git. First class, schmirst class.

It was a shame she couldn't tell the guy to go to hell, but that wasn't in her nature. She grew up in an environment of conflict, with warring parents and quarreling stepparents and combative step siblings. She'd become quite practiced at hiding her animosity toward anyone who pissed her off, and she would do so yet again now. But still, it irked her. Especially as she dragged her tired ass to zona quattro.

The gate agents announced that boarding was about to begin, and she stood helplessly and watched as Alexa and Mr. Romeo cruised right on to the Jetway. *Mr. Romeo*—as if. He was about as Romeo as, well, hmmm. Actually he was sort of Romeo-handsome. And he was tragic, in that his personality obviously sucked, so that fit into the whole Romeo thing. Maybe he'd swallow some poison over the loss of his first class seat. Isn't that what that Romeo guy did for Juliet? Then Stella could reclaim his seat on the plane. Did they serve strychnine on airplanes? She could send him a complimentary glass, on the rocks.

She stood there with the weight of her overloaded purse tugging on one shoulder, her computer bag on the other, watching as streams of people were being allowed onto the plane while her miserable zone-four line stood, constipated. It took forever but finally, they called her group, the last one, naturally, and passengers elbowed their way to get on board. As she wheeled her carry-on suitcase forward, a gate agent halted her right before scanning her ticket.

"I'm sorry, ma'am," she said. "You're only allowed one carry-on item."

Stella frowned. "Yeah. I know. And that's all I have—this suitcase."

The agent pointed at her shoulders. "What are those?"

"My laptop and my purse."

The gate agent pinched her lips shut and shook her head. She held up her pointer finger. "You're allowed one personal item. You're going to have to gate-check that suitcase."

Stella rolled her eyes. If she'd have just boarded before half the city of Milan got on the plane, no one would have breathed a word about that. But with all those people hauling all that luggage—most of them far more than she had—it figured they were going to run out of room for carry-on bags. Meanwhile she had all of her precious cake-decorating equipment in the suitcase, which she'd brought along to Florence in case of last-minute repairs to her cake. She couldn't afford to lose those supplies because she couldn't afford to replace them. This was her livelihood. But what could she do?

She heaved a sigh, grabbed the baggage-check ticket from the gate agent, and relented, handing over her luggage.

It wasn't till she was on the plane, her luggage long separated from her, that she remembered she'd tucked her breakfast into the rolling suitcase, in which she'd also stashed some of her favorite Italian cheese and salume. And wouldn't you know, when she arrived at her seat, she was sandwiched between a very large man, whose spread legs had spilled into her personal space by about five inches, and a child, whose middle name, she was sure, was "contagion," what with a whooping cough sound wheezing from his chest and a booger-encrusted nose that totally grossed her out to look at.

At the rate things were going, this day could only get better. Or at least that was the optimistic take she was going to try to pretend to believe.

The upside was minus the rolling luggage, at least there was no last-minute desperate search for enough overhead bin space to jam her supersized carry-on bag. But of course she had to wedge her laptop bag into a compartment in the far back of the airplane, which meant she'd have to wait for everyone else to get off the plane before she could walk the opposite direction of exiting passengers to recoup her bag. Lovely. Sleep was guaranteed to elude her for as long as humanly possible today.

Once she finally settled into her seat, she carefully inspected the safety card. If there was to be a crash landing, she wanted to know how to get out of this tin can in the air. Then, taking care to turn her head away from Typhoid Tommy next to her, she discovered the airline offered up a clever little app called Seat Chat, which allowed passengers to send messages to friends who were in other sections of the plane, using the screen in the headrest in front of them. If she couldn't sit next to Alexa, at least she could communicate with her. Far be it from that goon to have done the gentlemanly thing and offer his seat so that she could sit next to her good friend.

She pressed the screen and typed in the seat number she wanted to send to.

Hey, girl. It's me. Stuck in passenger hell between a diseased boy determined to take advantage of my sleep-deprived immune system and share his germy air with me and a space-violating man even more obnoxious than that cranky seatmate of yours, the blue-blooded Mr. First Class Jerk who kicked me out of line with you. What a douche. This guy next to me has, by the sheer dint of his size, taken over half my available space and I am not amused.

She paused for a moment and shoved back at the invasive man's leg that was closest to her before she resumed typing.

But getting back to that guy next to you—I mean seriously. Who died and made it his business where I stood or what zone I entered through? I hate arrogant men like that. If he was actually a nice man, he'd have done the gentlemanly thing and offered to switch seats so you and I could sit together. Instead I'm sure he's sitting there looking all hot with his bedroom eyes and ugh, I couldn't help but look—with Italian men and those tight pants, how could you miss it?—he was seriously packing.

Hope that thing doesn't get in the way of your seat. Ha ha! Now that makes me laugh—can you imagine him with his big old Italian Stallion cock spilling into your personal bubble? Alexa, honey, you'd best be careful or you'll be bitten by his love snake. In your personal bubble, no less. Omigod, that thought sends shivers down my spine. I needed a good laugh after the past few hours. Man, I'm so freaking exhausted. I cannot wait to burrow under my duvet and crash out for about twenty-four hours. By now I'd be napping happily were it not for the jerk with the big dick. Or is he the big dick with the big dick?

She snickered and the infectious boy next to her looked at her oddly.

Ugh, promise me you two won't fall in love in the next ninety minutes and then I'll have to be nice to him for the rest of my life and go to your wedding and feel compelled to admire the babies you make together even though every time I hold your child and stare into its eyes, I will be reminded of what a complete prick your baby daddy is. But you're too smart for that. Maybe when he's not looking, you can spit in his drink or something. I'd appreciate the passive-aggressive gesture on my behalf. Oh well, I wish I had one of those hospital masks to cover my nose and mouth against the crud little junior here is spewing my way.

She reread it and laughed again at her smart-ass comments. *Oh, God, Alexa will be peeing her pants cracking up at this message.* She hit the "send" button, put her seat in its upright position, and awaited takeoff, hoping the rest of the day would be drama-free and filled only with sweet dreams.

Chapter Two

DOMENICO Romeo was frazzled. First he missed his flight because he felt horrible watching the elderly woman trying to manage herself and her gargantuan suitcase at check-in at the airport. How could the poor woman not have anyone in her life to help her out? After watching her nearly fall in the parking lot and then twice drop her suitcase—the last piece of luggage on the planet without wheels, apparently—he had no choice but to offer his assistance. By the time he got her checked in and to her gate, they'd closed the doors to his plane and he was out of luck.

He waited at the airport for three hours for the next flight to Paris, choosing to relax with a cappuccino and two espressos at the coffee bar nearest his gate while catching up on the news. Eventually he settled into a comfortable reclining chair and listened to a fellow passenger who decided to sit down at one of those pianos that airports use to keep the flying public from becoming too animalistic when things got bad, which seemed to happen a lot these days. At least in America, from what he could see on the news. He figured Italians were too civilized to stoop to that sort of behavior.

That meant people needed to be respectful of the rules of air travel, and it was one of those pet peeves he had when people acted as if they were above those guidelines. Maybe it was a relic of growing up in a house with much mayhem after his father passed away. It seemed that some level of civility devolved after his father's unexpected death. Domenico was young enough to be powerless over how things unfolded, how each of his six siblings reacted to the loss of their father, some acting out badly, and how the light in his mother's eyes switched off overnight. It was then that he determined that rules would make him feel more safe and secure—structure, predictability. These things helped him fend off the fear that lurked deep in his soul about how life could change in an instant, and you'd be left with no control over the outcome.

His siblings fed him enormous amounts of shit for being this way. Lorenzo always said he had a stick up his ass. Valentina called him Domenico the Dominant. Ha ha. Francesco said he was uptight and needed to get laid. But that wasn't the problem—he'd had plenty of sex with a variety of women on a regular basis. Granted maybe it was a little overly controlling sex, and maybe that made the women he'd dated somewhat annoyed with him, but oh well. He needed control over things in his life. Period.

He heard an announcement that the plane would be boarding shortly, so he stood, grabbed his briefcase, and joined the queue already forming.

He hated waiting in those lines and wished like hell he could look forward to his customary first class seat where he could mind his own business and not be wedged into a tiny seat suitable for not much more than a chimpanzee. At six foot five inches, he couldn't bear the idea of being bent like a pretzel into those economy-class seats, uncomfortably tight as they were these days. Good thing it was only a ninety-hellacious-minute-long flight.

Meanwhile, the queue was filling up fast. He couldn't help but overhear the two women in front of him yammering on about some cake or something. Hardly a topic of conversation that appealed to him. One of them was petite with wide brown eyes and short dark hair that hugged her face. She was cute but not his type. He didn't go for the tiny ones. They seemed too fragile to him.

The other one had a gorgeous head of long, auburn waves, with sea-glass-green eyes. She was probably five foot nine inches tall, with a great athletic build: broad shoulders, narrow waist. Long, lean legs. Her red sundress with a halter strap tied at the back of her neck and showcased her ample tits perfectly, the chill air providing the added bonus of hardened nipples pressed against the flimsy fabric. He tried hard not to stare at them but wow, they were hard not to steal repeated glances at, mere inches away from him as they were.

He wanted so badly to talk to her, to get her name, her number, maybe ask her out for drinks. The more he thought about it, the more he needed to do it. But right when he was about to stir up the courage to say something, she caught him with his eyes laser-focused to her breasts. Busted.

He needed to say something, anything, so when he instantly diverted his gaze and noticed the boarding pass in her hand indicated she was supposed to be in a different line, he figured he'd point that out to break the ice. He couldn't have imagined she was going to practically jump up his ass with a hot poker. But no sooner did he say the words when her scowl told him all he needed to know about that potential offer of drinks.

What the hell? Here he was trying to save her getting yelled at when it came time to scan her ticket, and she instead freaked on him because she thought he thought she was cheating the system. Now it was true that he didn't care for people who didn't follow the rules, but he wasn't trying to be rude.

In hindsight, he should have known she wasn't going to be receptive when he pointed out she was carrying too much baggage. But he was only trying to help!

"They're not going to let you on with both of those," he said as he pointed at her many bags.

The look she threw him, with that telltale snarled lip, told him in no uncertain terms that if he asked her out on a date she would lop off his balls and serve them up, shish kebobbed, on a ceramic platter hand painted with his own blood.

Sometimes Domenico's tendency to live within the confines of societal expectations meant he could be socially awkward. Right now, he'd landed himself into social pariah territory, so he decided to quit trying so hard or he'd find himself with his dick tied in a knot and stuffed in his mouth if that woman had any say in the matter.

He exchanged pleasantries with the crabby woman's friend, Alexa, who, it turned out, was to be seated next to him. He'd been tempted to make everything right by offering to exchange seats with the woman to make amends, but he recognized hers to be a middle seat and there was no way in hell he could fit in one of those without panicking and demanding the cabin crew open the doors of the plane to let him off. Air travel could be claustrophobic enough in first class seating but downright torturous in cattle class, especially if you were tall.

Once in his seat, he was taking a few minutes to respond to some emails on his phone before they made him turn it off when the small TV screen in front of him dinged, and a notification in bold red letters appeared on the screen: *You've Got a New Message.*

A new message? What the hell did that mean? How does one get a message on a plane? And for what? He hoped it wasn't the airline revoking his seat and giving it to someone else. He had to be in Paris for a meeting in the afternoon.

As he sat there, perplexed, he saw the next screen come up, with instructions on how to access said message. He couldn't for the life of him imagine how he had a message when he didn't know a soul on this plane. Perhaps if he'd flown out of Florence he'd have recognized a couple of folks on the plane—it was a small enough world and his family's vineyard wasn't far from the city, but this time, departing from Milan had made more sense as it was a super-early flight and would give him the whole day in Paris. And he likely wouldn't have run into acquaintances here.

Had he known he'd have missed his flight, he'd have flown from Florence to begin with. Yet had he flown from Florence, he wouldn't have been late because he'd not have encountered the struggling old woman and felt compelled to help her out. Oh, well. Such is life.

He followed the instructions on the screen but had to stop midway because the flight attendants were going through those crash-and-die instructions no one pays attention to—the ones everyone would regret missing if something went awry with the plane's mechanisms. He tried to listen to be polite since they'd temporarily disabled the screen anyhow, but he was terribly distracted trying to figure out the message situation. Finally they shut up and he pressed the star key to retrieve it and began to read, realizing quite readily it wasn't meant for him since it started out with "Hey, girl."

What would be the protocol for something like this—an incorrect airplane mail message? He had no idea they had airplane mail messages. This was uncharted territory. Clearly someone sent it to the wrong person in the wrong seat.

Of course as much of a by-the-books guy as he was, he also was too damned curious to not continue reading. It fascinated him that he could communicate with strangers on a plane, and he tried to recall if there was anyone, in particular, he'd noticed in the gate area he'd like to chat up. There was that pretty woman who snarled at him, Alexa's friend, but no way was he touching her with a ten-foot pole. She would not be receptive to any overtures from him. In fact he wondered how long it took her to get on the plane—a glance back before he went through the gate showed that she was far, far from the front of the line. No doubt she was hurling invectives his way the whole time she cooled her heels in line.

He continued to read the missive: ...*the blue-blooded Mr. First Class Jerk who kicked me out of line with you. What a douche.*

Blue-blooded Mr. First Class Jerk? Whoever wrote this sounded awfully unhappy. And that douche thing. He always wondered about that word in reference to someone who is an asshole. Because if you think about it technically, it makes no sense. How is it that something intended for a woman to use when cleaning out her vagina would become a term for someone a person detested?

Who died and made it his business where I stood or what zone I entered through? I hate arrogant men like that.

Um… Hmmm. He paused to consider the chances. *Nah. Impossible.* It couldn't be her.

—he was seriously packing.

Whoever it was, she certainly went right for the kill. Did women actually talk like that? And did they actually do that—blatantly stare at men's crotches?

Can you imagine him with his big old Italian Stallion cock spilling into your personal bubble? Alexa, honey, you'd best be careful or you'll be bitten by his love snake.

Domenico's eyes grew wide. *Alexa, honey? Love snake?* Holy shit. It was from *her*—the mean girl. And she was talking about him! He couldn't believe a woman would have such a brazen conversation about a complete stranger via a messaging system on an airplane—what if you sent it to the wrong person? Which is exactly what she did. He tried to remember what row she was in. He'd read it out loud back at the gate. Was it fourteen?

Thank God he had the aisle seat and was tall, so he could strain to look toward the front of the plane to see if that was where she sat. He wanted to make eye contact with her, but dammit, he couldn't see a thing. He spotted a row he thought was hers: he noticed a little kid's arm hanging over the side. He could barely make out the top of her head in the middle and then a really tall man next to her.

By now I'd be napping happily were it not for the jerk with the big dick. Or is he the dick with the big dick? Ugh, promise me you two won't fall in love in the next ninety minutes and then I'll have to be nice to him for the rest of my life and go to your wedding and feel compelled to admire the babies you make together even though every time I hold your child and stare into its eyes, I will be reminded of what a complete prick your baby daddy is.

Well. No mincing words there. Clearly he'd made a bad impression. What was that saying about a woman scorned? Oh, yeah, hell hath no fury like one. Clearly that was the understatement of the millennium.

He pondered how to respond. Did he pretend he was Alexa? Except eventually she'd realize her friend had never received the messages and then she'd freak out wondering who had. Which would actually be awfully funny. But how could he pretend to be Alexa when he didn't know her, had no idea how to speak like her. He'd barely exchanged a handful of words with the woman. As he mulled over his options, the seat-back screen dinged, alerting him that yet another message had arrived. He assumed it was from his secret admirer because surely there couldn't be more than one passenger sending him missives.

Geez. It's taking you long enough to respond to me. Are you off in the lavatory with Bossy Big Dick Man? Maybe you've already discovered the joys of the Mile-High Club while I fester amid the fug of toxic, contaminated air up here with Billy Bacteria and Mr. Manspread, who I expect any minute to simply drape his giraffe legs on top of mine just to get more comfortable. What is it about men that they think they're more important than women? I'm sort of over it, you know? We've had our share of the whole "man's world" thing in pastry school. After all, everyone "knows" that the professional kitchen is a man's domain, right? I'm ready for women to take over the world, dammit.

Hmm, no wonder they'd been discussing cakes. He read on.

But seriously. I'm halfway jealous of you sitting next to that Italian dude. Sure, on the one hand, I'm pissed at him, but in truth, he was pretty easy on the eyes and right now my eyes could use something better to look at than Booger Boy. Have you talked to him? What was his name again? Domenico? Ha! Maybe we can call him Dominic the Donkey from that Christmas song, what with him being well hung and all. Although, hmm, do donkeys have big dicks? Or is it just horses? For that matter—what about zebras? And now that I'm thinking deep thoughts: are zebra cocks striped? Or solid? In which case are they black or white?

Domenico let out a snort. A zebra? A donkey? It was all he could do to contain himself.

I'd like nothing better than to hear you cackle right now, so I know there is something entertaining happening on this airplane somewhere. Just as long as the entertainment isn't you and Dominic the Donkey doing it donkey style in the tiny bathroom. Is there such thing as donkey style? I'll have to Google that when I'm off this godforsaken tin can. If it's anything like a horse—have you ever seen two horses going at it? Super violent. I feel awfully sorry for those poor mares. Although maybe they like those big horsey schlongs. I wish there was an emoji here for that cause I know you'd laugh if you saw that. A horse-sex emoji. Imagine.

She seemed a bit focused on the animal members, he mused, fighting another snort.

Hey—you up for going to that speakeasy tonight—the one in Saint Germain-des-Prés? I could kill for one of those cocktails we had there, with the grapefruit juice and bourbon and some other strange ingredients. Anything but that lousy wine I'm going to have to drink once classes resume. Ugh.

He stopped reading, a mixture of confusion and amusement floating through his head.

So she's in pastry school. Interesting. But she calls me Bossy Big Dick Man. I don't know whether to be insulted or flattered. Maybe she'd change her outlook if she got a firsthand look at it. Yeah, no. We'd be back to her lopping things off me, and that would not be a good thing. And what's with the "lousy wine" reference? Surely the woman doesn't hate wine? That would be downright insane. Not to mention uncivilized.

Domenico mulled over his options, then decided a course of action and hoped like hell the woman didn't have any sharp instruments on her. Little did he know that was a distinct possibility since she attended culinary school.

Chapter Three

STELLA was beginning to wonder if that stupid chat thing was working. Maybe she'd spent all that time composing her masterpiece messages to Alexa and they evaporated into cyberspace. She needed something other than Mikey McIllness next to her to occupy the rest of the flight time. Finally her screen indicated she had a message. *About damned time.*

Dear Alexa's friend (never did catch your name back at the airport), apologies from this section of the plane. Somehow we must have gotten off on the wrong foot. Although perhaps it's more like we got off on the wrong cock, judging by what seems to be your area of expertise. Based on your message to me, I'm presuming you have extensive knowledge about the male appendage, considering you write quite frequently about them. Mine, it seems, in particular.

Stella blanched. Had she sent her Seat Chat message to *him?*

Since you're so curious, I thought I'd elaborate a bit to—excuse the pun—"flesh out" the situation more. As in to distend, enlarge, tumefy, "make bigger." For one thing, something about this statement you made is not true: the big dick with the big dick. *I'll leave it to your imagination to determine which is false. But let's just say it's not the first time I've heard someone reference my "Italian Stallion cock." And not in a bad way. So perhaps it's in your best interest to learn more. And I will say you're the first person I've ever heard refer to me in that disparaging manner.*

No denying it. This was the guy. Instead of Alexa, her message had gone to the big dick with the big dick. Who was pretty much telling her she was correct about that certain physical detail. She swallowed and read on.

I don't suppose you'd give me another chance, and maybe if we're lucky, you'd have an opportunity to gauge for yourself whether indeed your musings about my endowment were spot-on or not. I for one would be happy to volunteer my services in the interest of civil discourse and in an attempt to make up for any misunderstandings back at the Milano airport. Perhaps we can have a drink in Paris? My treat. You can reach me at +39 0577 887766.

Key-rap. This was so not good. It was one thing to dish about the guy to Alexa, but oy vey. She never meant for *him* to see it. How did she ever send that to the wrong person?

She scanned back to where she sent the original message. She knew Alexa was in 27A. But argh, she clearly sent this to 27B. If she could shrivel up like one of those nighttime slugs she and her friends used to beg her mom to pour a beer over, she would. How could she ever face this man again? She was mortified. Except, wait a minute. As bad as this seemed, the fact was, she'd never have to see him the rest of her ever-loving life. Case closed. All was good with the world. She was going to be last off the plane anyhow since she'd have to retrieve her computer bag in the back. By the time she deplaned, he'd be long gone. Thank goodness!

She heard a ding. *Crapola.*

What's the matter? Cat got your tongue?

And the man must've found the elusive emojis she'd been unable to locate because he put a little kitty face on the end of it for emphasis.

She would simply pretend she never received the message. She'd keep her eyes forward for the rest of the flight, no more seat chatting, and pretend it all didn't happen. He'd get off the plane, she'd retrieve her laptop bag, and all would be right with the world.

It wasn't much longer till the flight attendant announced they'd be landing. After the plane taxied down the runway and parked at a gate, passengers did their typical scramble to grab their bags and queue up to get out of there. Stella, however, sat in her seat, enjoying the ability to spread out since her seatmates were both in the aisles already. She pulled out a nail file and cleaned up a few rough edges, relishing letting her elbows encroach on the other two seat spaces, counting her lucky stars she'd never see that man again.

At last the crowd started moving forward. Stella tried to keep an eye out for Alexa while making certain she made no eye contact with her nemesis. It was kind of weird watching the parade of passengers press past her—from her vantage point, it was a sea of hips and waistlines and hmmm, that man walking past had a pretty nice behind. Her eyes slowly scanned upward to see if the rest of him looked as good, only to realize too late that she was gaping at none other than the man she needed to avoid at all costs. She let out a gasp as he turned and waved and gave her a wink.

She thought she would die.

And following behind was none other than Alexa, who generously handed Stella her laptop bag.

"Hey! Luckily I was able to scoot back to get your bag and save you the hassle of working against the flow of traffic," she said, giving her a thumbs up as she passed it to her.

Stella gave her a wan smile. "Great." She practically winced as she said it. "Thanks a bunch."

Alexa stopped the line of passengers from inching forward to allow Stella into the aisle. Which meant she had the great misfortune of trailing none other than the very person she planned to never see or speak with again.

Domenico had spent the rest of the flight chatting with Alexa. He figured the best way to get to know something about that maddening woman in 14D who'd piqued his curiosity would be through discreetly pumping her good friend for information.

"So your friend—"

"You mean Stella?" Alexa shook her head in mock despair.

"Ah, so that's her name. Stella. Yes. So about Stella…"

"Please do forgive her for how she reacted back at the airport." She wrinkled her nose. "That's not how she normally is. She's been under a lot of pressure. We just finished up our exams and then she had this cake to make—"

"Cake?" He cocked an eyebrow.

"You see we're both in pastry school in Paris, at l'école Marondi. Stella loves to make and decorate elaborate cakes and she landed her first professional order for one—for a wedding in Florence. We're on our way back from there now—I went along to help with the cake."

His eyes grew wide. "What a massive undertaking. I can't imagine the number of hours it takes to create something like that."

"Well, it's what we've been training to do for months now. But Stella has quite a talent for wedding cakes—hers are far more beautiful than mine."

"I'm sure yours are amazing as well."

"Actually I'm more of a pastry girl, myself. If you're looking for an incredible croquembouche, I'm your gal," she said, referring to a tower of puff pastry balls stacked in the shape of a Christmas tree that are secured together with the finest strands of caramel. "I've got little interest in a future in wedding cakes. So much pressure."

He shrugged. "I can see that—people get uptight when it comes to weddings."

"Understatement of the year."

"So this friend of yours—I get the impression once she passes judgment there's no changing her mind."

Alexa laughed. "Wow, did you peg her." She nodded. "Don't get me wrong. Stella means well. But she can get a little hot-tempered. Couple that with lack of sleep and all those stress hormones coursing through her body and it's a recipe for being a little bit pissy."

"And how does one who might happen to be on the receiving end of that pissiness undo the damage?"

Alexa shrugged. "That is the million-dollar question. I've yet to figure it out. Maybe you can be the one to come up with the ultimate solution." She rifled through her purse and pulled out a piece of paper and a pen and scribbled something down. "Whatever you do, don't tell her I gave you this."

Domenico looked at the sheet of paper. It was a phone number. And next to it was the name "Stella" with this message: Good luck. And a smiley face.

He rolled his eyes. Good luck indeed. He had the feeling he was going to need all that and then some if he was ever going to make headway with this intriguing yet mercurial woman.

Chapter Four

STELLA couldn't believe her bad luck. How could Alexa have betrayed her like that, forcing her to walk right behind the man with whom she'd made a veritable fool of herself? Well, more a virtual fool. And in doing so, she could now hardly avoid breathing in how delicious he smelled. Sort of like a hike in the woods combined with a cozy fireplace on a cold winter's day, maybe throw in a chocolate lava cake for good measure. Damn, this was not good.

The worst thing was she didn't have tangible proof of what had transpired—it was all left behind in the black hole that was the airplane messaging system, curse them. So she couldn't go back to reread her messages to a) see how much of an idiot she'd made of herself and b) figure out if he was actually flirting with her or if he was simply mocking her in response. Not that it necessarily made a difference. She was absolutely not going to talk to him. She would make a beeline to catch the train into town and be done with him. That is, after she retrieved the bag they forced her to check thanks to him.

After what seemed an interminably long time, during which she went to great pains to avoid bumping into the guy—what was his name again? Romeo something?—they made it to the door of the plane, thanked the pilot for not killing them, and exited through the doorway, where Stella looked around immediately for her gate-checked bag.

There were about fifteen other small suitcases there, several that were dark gray like hers, but not a one had a pink ribbon tied to the handle as hers did. She sorted through the pile of bags over and over again as passengers continued to disembark, some of whom were retrieving their last-minute checked bags, and she barely noticed that the dick with the big dick had gotten involved trying to suss things out, and of course Alexa had as well.

"I need my bag," Stella said to the luggage guy who'd loaded the suitcases by the doorway. "I gave it to the gate agent in Milan. They told me it would be here." This man had supposedly taken them right from the belly of the plane onto where she stood on the jet bridge, so where else could her bag be but here?

He shrugged and handed her a slip of paper. "If your bag is missing, you'll need to fill this out and go to customer service."

"But you don't understand. I. Need. My. Bag. Surely it must be here somewhere. It has everything I need. Everything. My tips, my bags, all of my accessories."

The baggage guy only frowned at her.

"Sorry, *madame*," he said. "I cannot help you. Please." He motioned with his hand to usher her away from the airplane and toward the terminal. "This way and follow the signs to customer service."

It hadn't taken much for Stella's annoyance level to skyrocket. "Dammit," she said. "I need that suitcase. What the hell am I supposed to do?"

"It's okay, Stel," Alexa said, pressing her hands in front of her to motion for her to calm down. "We'll figure it out. If nothing else I can share mine with you."

"That's impossible. You know what it's like in class when we're making something new. We have to have everything right there, *mis en place*, in front of us at our station." She glared over at Domenico. "And thanks to that one, now I'm going to be totally hosed."

He looked at Alexa and shrugged his shoulders in a "what can I do" gesture.

"Would it help if I said I'm sorry for whatever it is I did that I don't know that I did and didn't mean to do, even if I didn't do it?" He sighed. "Better yet, is there some way I can help?"

She threw him the side-eye. "Thanks, but I think you've helped enough already." She threw her purse and laptop bag over her shoulders. "Look, Lex, I have to deal with filing a lost baggage form. You might as well hop a train back. At least one of us can catch some shut-eye."

Alexa knit her brow. "You sure?"

Stella nodded and shooed her away. "Go, get a start on your day. I'll be fine. Maybe we can meet up tonight. I'll message you."

Domenico realized right then and there that this was not going to be the appropriate place to communicate with

Stella. Instead he turned to Lexie for advice as she walked away.

"Look, I seriously am not sure what I did but I'd love to try to make things right. Can you let me know what she needs and I'll be happy to replace it? It's something I can easily afford and I'd be happy to try to cheer the poor woman up at this point."

Lexie stuck out her lower lip. "Honestly, it's not your circus, it's not your monkeys. She can figure it out."

"I understand that, but sometimes a kind gesture is all it takes to reverse a whole host of woes." He lifted his eyebrows to plead with her. He knew his bedroom brown eyes could warm up the coldest of souls. Then again, they hadn't done squat with Stella's. But surely her friend would agree to help him help Stella.

Alexa reached into a pocket of her purse, pulling out her phone. "Give me your number," she said, entering it into her phone as he read it aloud. After he finished reciting it, she used it to send him a text. "There. You've got my number, I've got yours. In case I forget, remind me to send you the list of supplies for our cake class—that's everything she had in that suitcase, so this way she'll be ready when classes resume. I'll even tell you the store where you can purchase the supplies in Paris."

"You're awesome," he said. "Now one last thing—speakeasies. Rumor has it there's one in Saint Germain-des-Prés that you two frequent."

Alexa grinned. "Prescription Cocktail Club. Rue Mazarine. Tell Mathéo at the door that I'm expecting you. We should be there by 22:00. I'll look for you." She gave him a brief nod. "Oh and we both love their *Le Mazarinette*. In case you're buying."

He nodded. "I'll take that under advisement. And, uh, any point sticking around here in the hopes that I can offer to share a ride into the city?"

Alexa shook her head. "Don't press your luck. It's going to take some doing to talk her off the ledge with you. Leave that to me."

His mouth lifted into a half grin. "Thanks. I think."

By the time Stella finished filing her claim and took the train back to her apartment, it was lunchtime. She was hoping to hit the pillows but instead she stopped at Paul, her favorite local boulangerie and patisserie and picked up a *raclette lardons*, an open-faced baguette with melted cheese and cubed, sautéed bits of bacon. She knew shouldn't waste money buying lunch and could make something equally delicious for less, but today, she needed to take the path of least resistance.

"It's about time," Alexa said as Stella opened the apartment door. "I've been waiting for hours to figure out what bee has been buzzing up your behind all day long."

Stella frowned. "You mean with that guy?"

Alexa nodded. "That wasn't exactly in keeping with the nonconfrontational Stella Whitaker I've known. Yet all of a sudden you were jumping all over that dude."

Stella held up her hands. "Ugh, was it that bad? I swear I didn't mean to do that. I'm not exactly sure what came over me." She dropped her bags and plopped down on the hot pink faux Victorian sofa they'd bought at a flea market for a steal. "It's just that he started telling me what to do and it seemed so, so, so impertinent!"

Alexa raised an eyebrow. "Impertinent?" She started to laugh. "How very Victorian of you, to go with the matching sofa you're sitting on, I suppose. I didn't know people used that word anymore."

Stella rolled her eyes. "Stop. I mean it threw me off. It was like he was dictating what I should be doing and that pissed me off. I guess it gave me flashbacks to my childhood or something, with my stepsiblings bullying me around all the time and that evil stepmother of mine. That sort of thing makes me bristle."

"I felt sort of sorry for the poor guy. He seemed baffled by whatever happened."

"Oh, Lex, you don't know the half of it."

"I can't imagine there was anything else other than what I witnessed."

"So let's say for a minute that I was stuck with annoying seat mates and I was in a sour mood and I was tired and cranky and then I discovered I could send you messages on the plane."

"What are you talking about?"

"Did you not see they had some messaging system?"

Alexa shook her head. "Honestly my eyes closed before the plane even took off. I slept for most of the flight."

Stella glared. "Don't make me hate you."

Lexie laughed. "I don't think you want to add to your enemies list, darlin'." She leaned in. "So tell me about this message thingy."

"Ugh, Lex, I sent this awful message to you that was intended to be funny but was super smart-ass, but I accidentally didn't send it to you. It was totally ragging about that guy. And the thing is, do you remember when we were standing at the gate? Did you happen to notice anything prominent about him?"

"Um, he was tall? Does that count?"

Stella shook her head. "It has to do with size, but not height."

Alexa squinted. "If you're saying what I think you're saying, I wasn't really looking there."

"Yeah, but that's because you're dating Antoine so you don't look that low anymore when you meet a guy."

Her friend burst out laughing. "I don't look that low? I mean, did I before?"

"Of course you did! Remember how we'd always laugh when we saw guys with tight pants on because you could immediately tell? And remember that one guy who had those loose pants but there was literally the worn-away outline in his crotch, sort of like how men's wallets create a permanent outline in the back of their jeans?"

Alexa grabbed the sandwich from her to mooch a bite. "All right, all right. Guilty as charged. I do remember that guy in particular."

"I mean what can I say? Sometimes you can't help but look there. And when I did, I noticed he was packing. And then I composed this witty note to you on the Seat Chat messaging thing and I sent it to you and finally you replied—it took forever, by the way—only it wasn't you who replied."

"Who was it?"

Stella turned beet red.

"No!" Alexa swatted her friend on the back, her eyes wide in amazement. "You didn't."

Stella hung her head. "Yup."

"So you wrote a message to me talking about the size of his package, only you sent it to him?"

"I mean, not only that." She finally looked up. "I did it in sort of a derogatory manner. Well, also complimentary, I suppose. I mean men love when people notice they're well hung, don't they? So I guess maybe he was flattered? But then again I sort of referred to him as the 'big dick with the big dick,' or something like that, which I'd imagine he probably didn't quite take as a compliment."

"Omigod, Stella! What were you thinking?"

Stella rested her face in her hands. "I seriously was so not thinking. I mean it was meant for you! It's something maybe you and I would joke about but you know I'd never say that to another human being!"

"What else did you say during your momentary lapse of sanity?"

Stella kept shaking her head. "The thing is, I don't know everything I said. I had no way to save it, you know? It was on the damned screen on the plane! I remember I made a lot of well-hung jokes. Some might have included things to do with horses. And donkeys." She hit her forehead with the palm of her hand. "Oh. My. God. I even invoked some stupid notion about calling him Domenic the Donkey because of his dong, and maybe I said something about doing it donkey style?"

"Donkey style? What the hell is that?" Alexa burst out laughing.

"I don't think it's a thing. Which is why I then started talking about horses having sex. I mean have you ever seen horses going at it? It's horrifying. You truly can't unsee it. After that, I may have speculated about zebra johnsons."

"Stella, Stella, Stella. You've done yourself a huge favor this time around."

Stella rolled her eyes. "Tell me about it. Thank goodness I'll never see the man again!"

Alexa squinted her eyes. "Uh, right." She pursed her lips. "Yeah. Thank goodness you won't ever see him again. That would be super awkward." She dusted off her hands as if that matter was taken care of.

Stella stood up. "Well, I feel much better getting that off my chest. I'm going to finally sneak in that nap I've been craving. You up for Prescription tonight? I could use an expertly made cocktail."

Alexa nodded. "Yes. Definitely. I think we're both going to need a couple of drinks under our belts by then."

Chapter Five

DOMENICO found a charming little Parisian bistro and dug into a plate of moules frites with a glass of bright, refreshing rosé from Provence. As much as he was Italian to the core, he loved the city of Paris, the food, and the people. Contrary to reputation, he did not find the French people the least bit off-putting and enjoyed conversing with Parisians he met along the way during his day. Besides, nothing like mussels and French fries to put him in a Parisian state of mind.

It was a lovely early summer evening, and he sat back and enjoyed a quartet of older men playing jazz on a nearby street corner as he ate his meal, mopping up every last drop of broth with pieces of baguette he tore right from the loaf. He remembered a French friend from university who told him the French referred to their daily bread as a *tradition*, not a baguette. He loved the funny quirks you discovered about different cultures once you got to know the locals.

He'd had a few meetings finalizing his plans for how he'd spend his time in the city and now was looking forward to trying to figure out that vexing woman, Stella the cake baker, at the speakeasy. He decided he'd arrive early and get a bead on the place, so he wasn't caught off-guard too late. He didn't want to show up, only to find some man hitting on her, which would completely blow his chances. Although he wasn't quite sure what his chances were. He was hoping her friend Alexa would throw him a lifeline if necessary.

After dinner, he enjoyed a cherry clafoutis—a sort of custard-like tart—for dessert. Man, did he love French desserts: worth the price of admission, and he savored every last bite. He then paid his bill, left a generous tip to the nearby musicians, and opted for a leisurely stroll along the Left Bank for the few blocks to Prescription. Twilight had begun to descend upon the city and the lights of Paris twinkled all around. It was such a magical city; it always felt ripe with the sense of possibility.

Domenico enjoyed people watching as he strolled along the Parisian streets—that and window watching. He encountered a shop that sold what looked like hand-hewn vestments for priests and royalty. Another window featured treasures from Katmandu. Interspersed along the way were stores with hipster French furniture and sexy French underwear. He stared at a subtly erotic bra, nothing fancy, just white lace but fairly sheer, one of those demi-cups that left you guessing, but only a little bit. He tried to picture the understated yet sexy bra on Stella but had to tamp down his imagination. He didn't want to show up at the bar "on display," since that would be awfully embarrassing under the circumstances. For the time being at least, he had to steer the conversation away from *that*.

He turned down Rue Mazarine and was glad he had the address on his Google Maps app because he arrived at a completely nondescript building on a street with a few restaurants and art galleries that were closed for the night.

There was no visible sign of what he was looking for but for a couple of men standing outside nearby.

"May I help you?" A short, wide, black man with a fedora hat and a snazzy pair of spats nodded at him.

Domenico checked his GPS again. "I'm pretty sure this is where I'm meant to be. Prescription? I was told to tell whomever that Alexa would be looking for me."

The man sized him up for a second, threw a glance to his friend who hopped onto a motorcycle, then turned back to Domenico and tipped his hat to him. "Enjoy your evening."

He pulled open an unmarked door and motioned for Domenico to enter the building, which instantly took him back in time. The place was intimate and cozy, darkly lit and inviting, in that let's-get-drunk-and-ignore-the-rest-of-the-world sort of way. He saw a flight of stairs that led to the upstairs, but he decided to remain on the main level in the hopes that Alexa would steer Stella toward the well-stocked bar there.

It was still early enough that he was able to get a seat at the bar, right in front of the bartender, a man who knew what he was doing with a cocktail. It was a perfect vantage point from which to watch his skills on display while also keeping an eye out for the entrance. He pulled up a stool and settled into the vibe of the bar. The bartender—who he learned was named Eric—plied his skills, magically producing concoction after concoction of colorful, fizzy, and foamy drinks, all of which made him want to sneak his finger through to grab a surreptitious taste.

Domenico took a look around him. Peppered throughout the Left Bank cocktail club were the usual suspects: hipsters with artfully crafted facial hair, a lot of men with too-small-by-design pants that ended about an inch above their shoes to allow you to see the wearer's deliberately clashing socks. Many, many tattoos. Sometimes places like this screamed pretentiousness, what with all the beautiful people milling about, but something about this place felt a little more comfortable than that. It didn't seem as if it was trying too hard. In fact, there was a handful not-beautiful people mingling and enjoying themselves. Who knew why the feel of this place worked so well—maybe it was Eric, a veritable conjurer who operated as if that cocktail shaker was an appendage he sprang from the womb attached to. All Domenico knew was that he was enjoying himself at this place. And the object of his interests hadn't even arrived yet.

Domenico ordered up a drink he couldn't pronounce but watched in amazement as Eric produced a frothy, happy-looking cocktail that could only put you in a good mood. As best he could discern, it contained some artisanal gin, maraschino cherry liqueur, absinthe (because what self-respecting Parisian cocktail didn't contain absinthe these days?), champagne, elderflower cordial syrup, fresh strawberries, and lemon juice.

He sipped his drink, which was going down awfully smoothly, and soaked in the jazz music mixed by a nearby DJ. He needed this chance to decompress a little. He'd found life at his family's vineyard, Cantine dei Marchesi Romeo, was stultifying. Sure he loved wine and without a doubt loved his family, but man, he needed a change of scenery. It didn't help that living cloistered on the family compound—one that had been in his family for some 600 years—sometimes made him feel like he was missing out on the rest of the world.

Yes, he resided in one of the most beautiful countrysides anywhere in the world. And he had access to the best of the best wherever, whenever he wanted. But from a day-to-day perspective, he was a grown man who basically lived at home. He'd been helping produce and promote his family's Chianti and other wines—some of the best Italy had to offer—for as long as he could remember. And he'd been running the events at the vineyard for years. He yearned for something more. Call it a premature midlife crisis or simply a desperate need for change. Which was why he decided to take some baby steps and come to Paris to do an intensive class studying French wines. Not that he was thoroughly uneducated about them, but he was immersed in his family's product, and of course he knew his competitors in Italy. Aside from that, well, it was sort of this gray area he never bothered with.

He'd been thinking more and more that he would love to be the one behind the stove at the vineyard, to be the person creating unforgettable meals for the various functions hosted at Romeo wines.

His family would likely think he'd gone mad wanting to put on a chef's toque and get hot and sweaty and end up with burns on his hands and arms and knife cuts all the time. Hence this small journey outside the family box. A way for him to declare some independence, to experience something a little bit different, and figure out whether he wanted or needed more.

For the umpteenth time today, he reflected on the day's events. It was weird that things started so strangely this morning. First helping that old woman, then missing the flight. Then that woman Stella going all ornery on him. He'd had more strange experiences in one day than he'd normally have in a six-month period if he simply stayed at the family vineyard or forayed into Florence or Rome for a day or two. Perhaps that's why he wasn't so terribly put off by Stella's anger. He'd been in a holding pattern for an awfully long time, so maybe having someone figuratively pounding on his chest wasn't such a bad thing after all.

Then again, perhaps he'd have to reserve judgment till after this evening. Because none other than Stella walked through the door in an adorable floral sundress, her hair pulled up in a ponytail, and by the look on her face upon seeing him, he hoped she wasn't prepared to upend a cocktail on top of his head.

"Eric—can you make me two of those Mazarinettes, and fast, please?" Domenico said, tossing extra cash on the bar as incentive.

He figured the only way he had half a chance was to ply this one with her favorite drinks, and quickly.

Chapter Six

STELLA didn't know whether to be furious or excited. Because there, smack-dab in the center barstool at her favorite bar in Paris was none other than the man she had planned to never see again. With good reason. Except that a tiny bit of her was curious to see him again for some bizarre reason. She decided her best course of action was to play it cool and see what was up. She'd had enough flying off the handle for one day.

Alexa was a few steps ahead of Stella and steering them toward the Italian man right as Eric slid two of her favorite drinks toward him. Which was curious that he would know what that was. Maybe it was merely a wild guess. Or maybe there was some collusion between a certain friend behind her back... who she probably couldn't even blame.

Before she had a chance to say a word, Domenico stood up, extended his arms to proffer his seat and the one next to it to them, offered a traditional Italian two-cheek kiss to both women, then handed them each a drink. With a nod, he lifted his own glass and offered a toast.

"*Salute*," he said. "Or perhaps I should say, *à votre santé*. When in Paris, after all."

Stella nodded slowly, trying to figure out how to respond, and took a large slurp of her drink. "Okay... I'll play along. So you knew I'd be here because?" She looked at Domenico and then at Alexa, who seemed to be squinting at him. Yet who knew if her friend was trying to send a coded message to the man, or maybe she had something in her eye? Yeah, right.

"In the flurry of communications between us all"—he pointed at both women as well as himself—"you must have forgotten to mention showing up at Prescription tonight."

She blanched. Dammit, her big fat blabbermouth. Or blabberfingers, since she had typed that rather than spoken it to him. This would teach her to be so sloppy in sending messages. She smiled weakly. "About that—"

He held up his hands to stop her. "No need for further discussion. I get that it was an accident, and what transpires between friends is your business... I happened to be an unwitting witness." He grinned.

Stella groaned and buried her face in the palm of her free hand—after taking yet another swig of that tasty drink.

Alexa set her drink down. "My, my. Where are my manners? I forgot to do formal introductions." She winked at Domenico. Stella stuck her tongue out at her. "Domenico Romeo, scion of a legendary wine empire in Tuscany, I'd like you to officially meet my good friend Stella Whitaker, an amazing cake baker, who I promise is not usually quite so offensively loose-lipped. Or should I say forked-tongued? At least not with strangers."

Domenico bent forward and lifted her hand to his lips. "*Enchanté, mon cher.*"

Lovely to meet you, my dear.

Stella rolled her eyes. This guy was laying it on thick. But she'd promised Lex she'd behave tonight, so she was simply going to fake it in order to make everyone happy. And maybe because his eyes kind of seemed like they were boring holes into her soul. On the one hand that seemed sort of invasive but on the other, it was kind of hot. How could he make her feel so stripped down with one partial sentence in French? She hated to see what would happen if he started speaking Italian to her—she'd be a goner.

She took another swig of her drink, only to realize she'd finished the thing in three gulps. This was going to be an expensive night if she kept up at this rate.

Domenico motioned to Eric for more drinks, which soon materialized in front of them. Expensive for him, it seemed.

Alexa pulled out her phone and held it up to her ear, motioning to her friend that she needed to take a call. Stella made a mental note to throttle Lex when they got home for abandoning her in her time of need.

Domenico settled on the barstool next to Stella. She could feel the solid warmth of his thigh against her bare leg, and it unnerved her.

He turned toward her and smiled. "So now that we officially know each other yet have to pretend that we haven't already communicated, where do we go from here?"

Nothing like calling a spade a spade.

Stella took a deep breath. "Hell if I know. I usually keep my head down and focus on my work—I don't normally tend to get into big kerfuffles with strange men."

"Kerfuffles?"

"It's some sort of slang. Maybe it's from the English. It sounds like a word they'd come up with. It means hoopla, a commotion. That sort of thing."

"Hoopla. Okay. You've got a far more extensive English vocabulary than I do."

"What I'd love to hear is something Italian."

He arched a brow. "You like Italian?"

She shrugged. "Everything sounds better in Italian."

"Bellissima, mi abbaglia con la tua bellezza."

"Did you just say that I have a head like a rhinoceros?"

He shook his head. "I said that you dazzle me with your beauty."

Stella blushed. "But scare you with my words?"

He tipped his head and fixed her with his gaze. "I must admit you gave me pause." He took a sip of his drink. "Perhaps on a different day I might have been more offended, but it's been a strange sort of day for me, so it seemed perfectly fitting."

"And I contributed to your strange day?"

"I'd say it's more like you were the highlight of it."

She rested her hand on her chin and looked at him. "I suppose I'll take that as a compliment." It was weird. All of a sudden she was starting to enjoy this man's company. It truly was a strange day. Either that or this liquor was going to her head more than she realized.

Of all the times she'd been to Prescription and gotten into conversations with men, never had she felt as attracted to one as she did to him. It made absolutely no sense whatsoever. Just because he was charming meant nothing. He lived in Italy. She was going to school in Paris. After that, who knew what would happen—her visa wouldn't last forever, so unless she found steady work and was able to change her visa accordingly, she'd be stuck returning to the States, to her provincial little Pennsylvania town, with no job and no aspirations, which would be a bit of a letdown after living in such a magnificent city. It was as if Paris had spoiled her for life.

But if she was stuck returning home after this, then perhaps she should make the most of what she could while she could. She looked at the handsome man sitting next to her: his inviting eyes, those thick lashes. That hair she could imagine running her fingers through.

What was it he said to her in that message? Something to the effect of 'if we're lucky, you'd have an opportunity to gauge for yourself whether you were right about me?' Was he serious about that? Better yet, was he volunteering his services for the cause? She shook her head. Of course he was. What self-respecting man wouldn't offer himself up. Hardly self-sacrifice. More like self-serving. But then again, He was hot. And, despite her earlier impression, he was nice. And courteous. And seemed genuine. And, well, it was hard to argue with that other bit.

"So, Domenico," she said, bracing herself to delve further before she would make up her mind about things. "You're into wine?"

Chapter Seven

DOMENICO could hardly believe the change in demeanor in this woman. What a difference a half a day made! After the episodes this morning, he could never have imagined he would be sitting here, so close their shoulders practically touched, conducting a civilized conversation. Weirder still that he was marveling at such a thing. It wasn't usual for Domenico to be the pursuer; normally women were more than happy to go after him. One thing was for sure: Romeo men didn't have any trouble finding willing women. Maybe that was part of the intrigue with Stella—that she wasn't like those other women.

He tried to imagine what it would be like to be in a relationship with someone like her. Fiery, hot-tempered, hard to predict. On the one hand, that might drive him crazy. On the other hand, it might be interesting. And if she was like this out in the open, imagine what she'd be like in bed. That thought made his cock stand up and take notice, which he tried to mentally tamp down because he was trying to avoid going there with her right now. He was happy they'd steered the conversation to mundane things, versus body metrics, or whatever you'd call her fixation on size.

"Yes, wine is sort of synonymous with the Romeo name," Domenico said. "My family's winery has been run by Romeos since the Middle Ages."

Stella's eyes grew wide. "Wow. My family's history goes back to, oh, I think the Eisenhower administration. If that."

He laughed.

"But seriously, that's one of those things about Europeans—they seem to have such a strong hold on their legacies. They have these roots that go so deep and it's something each generation works to preserve. I admire that so much. For that matter, it does make me jealous. There's nothing compelling to unearth where my family is concerned except if you want to hear about a few ugly divorces and some unplanned pregnancies." She shook her head.

"I'm sure there is more to your family than you realize," Domenico said. "Sometimes we aren't that interested in delving into the past to learn about it."

She shrugged. "Yeah, not much to sink your teeth into. My mother got pregnant with me when she was sixteen. Her parents forced her to marry my dad, who was miserable. Eventually he ditched her, took up with a dragon lady who I'm pretty sure laid eggs rather than gave birth to children, and I was stuck dealing with the fallout from them all. Oh and then my dad left her too. And my mother is an alcoholic and I try not to deal with her. End of story."

"*Mi dispiace*," he said as he placed a hand over hers. "I'm sorry. That doesn't sound like an ideal environment in which to grow up. How did you end up in Paris? Were you running away?"

She knit her brows. "Running away? Interesting way to look at it. Maybe in a way, I was. But I like to think of reaching toward a goal rather than fleeing from something. Although they are perhaps two sides of the same coin."

"But what was in Paris?"

"Besides the usual things—good food, beautiful scenery, amazing history? Now I'm going to get deep: I spent much of my childhood feeling very alone. The one thing that brought me joy was baking. Whenever I could scrape together enough money for supplies, I would bake something. I didn't have anyone to make it for. I swear I would go to my neighbors' houses and leave things on their porches. Eventually they learned it was from me and started asking me for more. At some point, a teacher planted the idea in my head that I should go to pastry school. Until then, it was not even something I knew they had. Schools where you bake? Sign me up!"

"Sounds fantastical, doesn't it?"

"Like you wouldn't imagine." She sipped her drink. "I used to daydream about this all the time. And then one day I decided I was wasting my life, working at lousy minimum-wage jobs, going nowhere. I couldn't stand to be under the same roof as my stepmother, who loved to blame me for her own problems. I knew that even if it meant incurring lots of debt, which I couldn't afford, at least I would be buying myself a life. So I applied to school and the next thing you know, I was on a plane, Paris bound."

"The only place better would have been Italy bound." He winked at her. "Though I admit to being partial."

"So what is it you do for your family's winery? I have to admit I know nothing about wine. I'm a mixed-drink or beer girl. Wine does nothing for me."

He cocked an eyebrow. "Then you've not had the right wine. I can assure you if you tried our Chianti Classico Riserva you would fall in love." He scrunched his forehead. "With the wine, of course."

"Of course. After all, your wine isn't some sort of weird love potion."

He smiled. "Perhaps in a small way it is. At least to me. Maybe it's more like a love letter of sorts, to the soil, to the sun, to the generations of Romeos who have worked to perfect it."

Stella squirmed in her seat a bit. She was getting uncomfortably charmed by this man. It was like he was a damned poet or something. "Thanks, but I'll stick to my Prescription cocktails. Nothing cures what ails you like one of Eric's surprise concoctions."

Domenico shrugged. "Well, the offer stands. If you'd like to indulge in a little bit of Romeo, I'm your man."

Indeed he would be her man. If she were to indulge in a bit of Romeo. But that was so not on her agenda, and besides, it was getting late and she was getting drunk.

"Thanks, I'll keep that in mind." She glanced at the time on her phone and looked around for Alexa, who was nowhere to be found. "I think I've been stood up. By my own damned roommate." She typed a quick text to her friend to find out when she'd be back. Her phone dinged immediately.

"Sorry, didn't I tell you? I had to leave to go pick up Antoine since he got out of work early. I'm spending the night at his place…"

Stella frowned. "Dot, dot, dot. Curse her."

Domenico cocked his head to the side. "Dot?"

Stella shook her head. "Lexie. She's making a lot of presumptions, and suffice it to say I'm going to give her a serious piece of my mind the minute I see her."

"War is not the answer." He grinned then motioned to Eric for two more drinks.

Stella held up her hands. "Seriously, if I have another drink I will be incapacitated. Which is probably what my roommate would wish for."

"After the day you've had, I'd say it's precisely what the doctor would order. And you are, after all, at Prescription. Take one more drink and then we'll talk about it in the morning."

Stella was trying to figure out if Domenico was playing with her or not. He hadn't made any advances, which got her thinking that maybe this was all a make-nice-over-drinks thing and they would go their separate ways and be done with it. She hoped that's what it was from his perspective. Although the longer she sat with him, the more she'd started to entertain thoughts about the man. After all, he was actually fairly friendly. And easy on the eyes. And he filled out his pants so nicely. Not that that was a prerequisite or anything, but, hmmm… It had been quite awhile since she'd had fun with a guy. School was so demanding, and then she had that wedding cake job. For that matter, she hadn't gone out and had fun of any sort for ages, let alone dabbled with a boy. Classes didn't start for another day, so she had nowhere to be tonight.

Eenie, meenie, miney, moe… This was awfully tempting to contemplate. She took a sip of her drink, licking the excess from her lips, and had an idea.

"How do you feel about tangoing?"

Chapter Eight

DOMENICO could barely move his gaze from Stella's mouth. Her pink tongue peeked out and followed along her lips, licking every last bit of the drink from her mouth. He couldn't stop thinking about what he wanted to do with that tongue, and it was making him crazy. So when she asked him what he thought about tangoing, well, naturally his mind went straight to the gutter. He beamed at her. And Stella pulled up her phone and typed something into it. He had no idea what but hoped it was a text to her roommate to not come home till noon.

"And by tango, do you mean what I think you mean?" He quickly slid his credit card to Eric to close up the tab. As soon as he'd approved the charge and left a fat tip on the bar, he looked at Stella, whose hand was reaching for his.

She pulled him out the door of the bar and into the warm Parisian night air. They walked down to the corner where she waved her hand at an approaching car, then opened the door and stepped into an Uber. Domenico barely contained his joy that—barring unforeseen circumstances—he was going to get lucky with Stella Whitaker. He could not think of a better ending to this day.

Except that the Uber pulled over right as they approached the River Seine, and Stella quickly thanked the driver as she got out at the Quai Saint Bernard. Domenico duly followed. It sure didn't look like there was an apartment nearby. She pulled him along as they walked down a ramp onto a cobbled path toward an urban sculpture garden that led to a miniampitheater of sorts along the edge of the river.

The Bateaux Mouches open-air boats glared their lights at nearby picnickers enjoying food and wine and a lovely night in Paris. More people were camped along the Île Saint-Louis with picnics spread out as well. The Gothic beauty of the Notre-Dame Cathedral loomed nearby on the Île de la Cité.

Dusk fell late in Paris in the summertime, so the sky was just morphing from twilight into darkness. The lights of the city reflected in the water and the splash of waves as boats moved up the river lent a musical quality to the air. But the waves weren't the only melodious interludes as they quickly approached a gathering of hundreds of people in and around the amphitheater moving to the beat of Argentine music.

"This is one of the many things I love about Paris," Stella said, pointing toward the couples entangled in the tango. "Every night people come out here to dance." She nodded toward another nearby amphitheater, where people were doing swing dancing. "People of every stripe, from all over the world. Some are couples who came here together, but many are strangers who simply love to dance—they show up with their dancing shoes to find a partner and share the joy of the moment. There are men in turbans, women in saris, others in dreadlocks, and some in bare feet:

people of many nationalities, happily joined together in dance."

"So, um, by tango, you meant actual dancing?"

She laughed. "Of course. What else could I have meant?" Stella's emerald eyes sparkled with mischief, and he was attracted to her even more. She could be an imp, it seemed. Which was okay. He could play this game. And lucky for her, he could also dance.

"All right, then." He extended his arm and her hand clasped his as he pulled her toward him into an embrace. They picked up the dance in the midst of the large crowd of dancers. "The gauntlet has been thrown."

There wasn't a lot of room for anything too elaborate, but it didn't matter. Being this close to Stella far exceeded Domenico's expectations, so this was all icing on the cake. It didn't hurt that he was a fairly decent dancer—something he'd picked up while at university when he realized how much women loved it.

They moved together easily, and when the song changed, they stayed there dancing, rather than stepping back into the crowd of observers.

"I have to say I'm impressed with your tango skills," Domenico said.

"Would it shock you to know that I picked this up by coming here as frequently as possible?"

He nodded. "All the more admirable. It's not the easiest dance to learn. How did you find out about it?"

"Lexie's boyfriend, Antoine, took us here the first time, when the weather turned and spring announced itself. We brought a picnic and sat on the steps and I simply couldn't keep my eyes off people doing the tango, it's such a gorgeous and sensual dance," she said. "Yet you have in mind these gorgeous, lean, professional Argentine dancers but instead it's normal people from all walks of life. Sometimes the old man dressed in shoddy clothing who looks as if he's a vagrant will be the most talented tango dancer out there. And I love that people show up alone, slip off their street shoes, and pull on a pair of heels made exactly for this. I guess it intrigued me that some average nobody like me could learn to dance like that."

He shook his head. "I beg to differ with you but I'd hardly call you an average nobody. You're soon-to-be-famous baker Stella Whitaker."

She scrunched her nose. "Thanks for the vote of confidence. You sure you're not trying to butter me up?"

"I've been trying to butter you up all day long but see where that got me," he said with a laugh. "Right now I'm just being honest."

Stella blushed and looked away at the same time Domenico tried to do a stop with his foot when she was expecting to do a leg wrap. Instead she tumbled in what seemed like slow motion but was decidedly quick, landing amid a thicket of tangoing legs and feet, her leg half-twined around Domenico's still, her cute floral dress hiked up over her waist, her insanely sexy hot pink thong the only thing he could focus on for a fleeting moment, before he dope-slapped himself and quickly scooped her up and carried her away from the crowd of dancers.

"Oh my God, Stella, I'm so sorry. Are you okay?" He'd motioned for some spectators to scoot down on the stone amphitheater bench so that he could set her down and get a look at the damage. He settled in next to her with her legs draped over his as he checked out her ankle, which was swelling up angrily.

Stella rolled her eyes. "Ugh. I can't believe I fell ass over tea kettle in front of all those people."

"I am so sorry. I shouldn't have put my foot down just then."

She waved her hand dismissively. "Please. That wasn't your fault. I was the one trying out the fancy move. Rookie mistake. Totally my fault."

"Let's agree to split the blame fifty-fifty, then." He gently lifted her foot and pressed where a bruise was starting to blossom on the outside of her ankle. He undid the strap of her sandal, sliding the shoe from her foot. God, he'd much rather have removed that under far more alluring circumstances, maybe after having stripped her naked and taken a good, thorough look at her in only the thong and those strappy heels.

"We need to get you back to your place and get some ice on this," he said. "What's your address?"

He pulled out his phone, opened up his Uber app, and called for a ride. Then he rolled up his sleeves and lifted Stella into a seated position cradled in his arms as she wrapped hers around his neck. He carved a path through the crowd and carried her to the very spot where they'd been dropped off by Uber earlier. Flagging the driver, he motioned for him to pull up and loaded Stella in across the back seat as he climbed into the front seat.

Twenty minutes later, they were in front of her building in Belleville. He helped to ease her from the car, and she buzzed them in through the ancient oak doors that opened to one of those lovely secret cobblestoned courtyards that are so ubiquitous in Paris. He momentarily set her down then turned to see three doors that led to three separate apartment buildings. "Which is yours?"

Stella pointed at the one behind them. "But I'm afraid it's not good news. I'm four flights up."

He lifted an eyebrow. "No elevator?"

She shook her head. "But seriously, you've done enough. I can get up the steps. I'll be fine."

He opened his eyes wide. "Are you kidding? You're not fine and I'm going to make sure I get you into your apartment safe and sound."

She shrugged. "Fine, but please don't carry me. Maybe I can lean on you while I hold onto the railing?" She winced as she tried to put weight on her foot.

"Don't be ridiculous," he said. "I've got this."

Stella sighed and let him pick her up yet again. "I owe you for this."

Domenico smiled. If only he could actually cash in on that IOU, he'd be a happy man.

Chapter Nine

IT was after two in the morning when they finally entered her apartment. Stella felt like a huge pity project and hated that Domenico was wasting precious sleep time lugging her ass around.

She opened the door and looked around for signs of her roommate, but clearly, she'd indeed opted to evacuate the place for the night. Which would have made this moment awkward except now that she was the walking wounded, it probably precluded anything else from unfolding. Bruised ankles and hookups didn't go hand in hand.

"Let me get some ice on this thing," Domenico said as he opened the small refrigerator. He grabbed a nearby dishtowel and placed a handful of ice cubes from the tray into it, fisting the towel into a ball and gently pressing it on her ankle. She was stretched out on the pink sofa, hating being even remotely incapacitated. That was not how she preferred to operate.

"You've done far too much already. And it's so late. I give you permission to unburden yourself of any perceived obligations to me so you can go catch some sleep."

But he was not planning to leave anytime soon judging by the way he was moving down the hallway, scouting out the place.

"So you share a room with Alexa?" he said as he poked his head into the bedroom.

"Well, yeah. It's Paris. We're poor students. We were lucky to get a bedroom."

"And you share a bed as well?"

She sighed. "I know, right? It's fine except when her boyfriend comes over and I'm relegated to the sofa, which actually converts into a futon of sorts, so it works. I'm guessing you don't have the same problems where you live?"

Domenico laughed. "Not exactly," he said. "Although if it's any consolation, I still live in the same house I grew up in, but it's not actually a house. It's a bit more, well, spacious than that."

She raised her eyebrow. "Spacious?"

He held up his hands in surrender. "Okay, so it's an Italian palazzo."

Her eyes grew wide. "You live in a *palace*?"

"Does it help if I remind you that I live at home?" he shrugged. "I mean it's not my palazzo. It's been in my family for hundreds of years. So we all live there. It's kind of what's been done with the Romeos. For what seems like all of eternity." He frowned.

"Do you have any privacy there?"

"That can be complicated to answer," he said. "I mean it's a big place, so it's not as if anyone else can hear what goes on in my room. But there are times I could be bringing someone home and we happen upon my mamma doing her needlework in the great room. Now *that* can be awkward."

Stella laughed. "I bet your mamma knows everything that goes on in that house."

He nodded. "She is omniscient, no doubt about that."

"So do you like living there?"

He raised his hands up in a sign of ambivalence. "Am I feeling stifled? You bet. Do I adore my family? Absolutely. Do I need some space although I live in a home that's bigger than this building? Weirdly, yes."

"At least you aren't stuck listening to your roommate and her boyfriend having sex four nights a week."

"Oh, I don't know. That could be fun." He wiggled his eyebrows and poked her in the ribs to tease her.

"Thanks, but I'll take a pass on that. The only upside is this building is ancient and the walls are pretty thick."

"I take it Alexa's out for the evening, then?"

Stella nodded.

"In that case, let's get you ready for bed so you can enjoy a night in your own room."

He helped her down the hall and into the room and sat her on the large bed.

"Okay, where are your pajamas?"

She frowned. "I sleep in my underwear." She blushed as soon as she said it and needed to explain herself. "No air conditioning in this place—it gets hot!"

"In that case, I guess I'll help you get into bed and then I'll be off."

Stella frowned. She didn't exactly want him to "be off." She'd had a fun night, and like she was thinking earlier, what the hell? Domenico was cute and sexy and sweet. Maybe a little playtime was in order. She could work around that bruised ankle.

She extended her leg. "Would you mind taking off my other sandal before I slip under the sheets?"

Domenico looked at her leg and smiled. "If you insist." He leaned over and began to unbuckle the strap, then slowly pulled the shoe from her foot, dropping it to the ground. As he continued to hold her foot, he looked up and his jaw dropped. Stella had pulled her dress over her head, leaving her naked but for a hot pink bra that matched the thong she'd already revealed to him, albeit under awkward circumstances. "Um, would you like me to tuck you in?"

Stella grinned. "Is that what they call it these days?" She crooked her finger and Domenico let go of her good foot, immediately inching his way toward her on the bed.

"It?" he said, his breath coming faster.

She pointed at him and then at herself. "When a man and a woman find themselves alone together and one is nearly naked and the other has entirely too many clothes on." She popped the front hook of her bra and shrugged out of it quickly, then leaned forward and began to unbutton his shirt, the crisp, starched cotton yielding beneath her fingers. She tugged his shirttails from his waistband and reached her hands to either side of his collar, pulling him toward her until they were chest to chest, and her lips barely grazed his.

"But what about your ankle?" He placed his large, warm hands on her waist.

"I'm pretty sure the best course of action is to get my mind off of it." She slid her hands over his shoulders and pulled off his shirt. "I'm afraid I might need to lie down to relieve the pressure."

He groaned.

"Although it looks like I need to help you relieve some pressure first." Her fingers went to his pants and she unfastened the belt from its buckle, deftly unbuttoning and then carefully unzipping the pants, before she fell back against the pillows, pulling him down against her. "There. How's that?"

"Fucking unbelievable," he said as he settled his mouth over hers, first softly but then with more pressure, his tongue pressing along the seam of her lips so that she opened to him. They both groaned as their tongues met, taking turns stroking, licking, and tangling with one another.

Domenico's hands skimmed along Stella's body until finally, his thumbs found her nipples, which he pinched and massaged till they were hard points. It was Stella's turn to groan. She got even by pulling him closer, pressing her hands on his ass, so that his swollen cock urged itself against the juncture of her legs.

"You have entirely too many things on still," Stella said between kisses, her hands sliding beneath his briefs and skirting them off his ass. Domenico took over and pulled his pants and briefs off, tossing them to the floor as he nudged her legs apart and settled himself between them. He kissed her nose. "There. How's that."

"Much better." She ground her hips against him and he let out a low growl as his lips found their way around her face, her chin, down along her throat, her breasts, and finally settled on a nipple.

Stella bit her lip and moaned, it felt so amazing. It seemed like forever since she'd done this with a man. What on earth had kept her from it? Other than she didn't want to start something when she wasn't going to be able to finish it. But who said she couldn't start and stop it all in one day? She could happily have this little fling with him and get back to normal tomorrow. He was only visiting Paris anyhow. It's not like this could go any further. So what was wrong with the here and now? *À la minute,* to filch a French culinary terminology.

Stella closed her eyes and let herself sink into the sensations, his warm, wet tongue licking and sucking on her nipple, his teeth occasionally nipping the tip. If she was going to live for the moment, she was going to enjoy the hell out of it. And tomorrow? Well, she'd cross that bridge when she got to it.

Chapter Ten

DOMENICO wanted to make this last. He hadn't been with a woman in quite a while. Somehow the distractions of his little life crisis seemed to have put women on the back burner. At the moment he was trying to understand how he'd made such a terrible lapse in judgment because shit, being pressed flesh to flesh with the soft, warm curves of this woman was about to make him come prematurely if he didn't get a handle on himself.

He looked up at Stella as if for guidance. Her eyes were momentarily closed but she seemed to be in a state of pleasure, her lips parted in a smile, her cheeks flushed, so he took that as silent approval. He shifted himself down her body, nipping and licking and sucking and biting as he trailed his mouth along her soft belly and her hips, meandering his way toward that thong he couldn't wait to rid her of. He pulled on the thin straps at her hips and discarded it quickly, then traced his mouth down her bare mound, his tongue finding her clit and circling it teasingly. Stella cried out and he paused to catch her eye. She smiled, a look of bliss on her face, and he winked at her and used his tongue to trace a long lap along her lips, already moist with her juices. He moaned. How he was going to last was hard to fathom.

With both hands, he parted her lips and took his time savoring the view before inserting first one then two fingers inside her, hooking them forward to press toward that elusive G-spot, which he knew would bring her to climax. He took long, wide strokes of his tongue along her wet center, occasionally circling her swollen clit, his fingers moving at a steady pace deeper inside of her.

Stella's breath was coming faster and her hips gyrated to the rhythm of his hands pumping into her body. With a loud moan, she suddenly held still, her body shuddering as she coaxed her orgasm to conclusion. Domenico sat up, licked his lips, and locked eyes with her.

"Please tell me you have something," she said, a pleading look in her eyes.

He reached for his pants, pulled a condom from his wallet, and repositioned himself between her spread legs.

"You're killing me with that view, you know." He grinned.

"You're killing me with that hard-on, you know," she said, laughing.

"Does it meet with your approval? I know you'd made some presumptions based on, shall we say, external evidence."

She laughed. "Oh my God. Will I never live that down?" She pulled him toward her and pressed her mouth to his, dragging her lips, lapping up what remained of her juices.

"Fuck, Stella, that is such a turn-on."

"You ain't seen nothin' yet." She pushed him backward against the mattress and straddled one of his legs as she took her turn trailing her mouth along his chest, stopping to nip at his nipples, tracing her tongue along his hard abs, and following the happy trail of hair that led to her ultimate destination. She wrapped a hand around his swollen cock and pressed her tongue to the tip before closing her lips around the head and sucking him hard.

Domenico thrust his hips toward her mouth and pressed his hands to her hair, not wanting his cock to lose a second of contact with her warm, soft mouth. He pumped into her as she took as much of his cock in as she could until he couldn't stand it another second and pulled out.

"How do you want it, baby?" he said as he rolled the condom on, not wanting her to be in a position that would hurt her ankle.

She made the decision for him as she spread her legs across his hips and settled herself over his cock, slowly sinking onto it, inch by slippery inch. They both gasped as he filled her, and their bodies were finally pressed to one another. He stilled, savoring the sensation.

Stella rotated her hips in a grinding motion, her wet body sliding against his pelvis, and Domenico about died. "Stella, you're killing me," he said as she rode his cock, pulling away till they almost separated, then allowing him to spear her again with his hard length. He pulled her closer so he could latch on to her nipple, which made her move faster against him, her breathing short and hard as she rode him to another orgasm. He gave her a few seconds as her muscles tensed and squeezed against his cock and carefully flipped her, his body covering hers as he braced himself and thrust his cock into her. He picked up the pace and she spread her legs, clutched his ass, and pulled him toward her. Finally with one hard thrust, he pressed himself deep into her wet pussy and let out a loud yell as he came hard, his cock pulsating inside her body, his hips twitching as he emptied himself into her.

Domenico could hear the shout of the street sweeper four stories up as he stirred right before dawn. He grabbed his phone from the nightstand where he'd left it hours earlier, and saw a calendar alert pop up that he had a breakfast meeting in exactly one hour. Which meant he had to get all the way back to his hotel in the sixth arrondissement and if he didn't leave now, he'd be stuck in crazy rush hour traffic and never get back in time to change and make his breakfast.

He glanced over at Stella, who was beautiful in her peaceful sleep. He hadn't the heart to wake her only to leave. Instead he dressed quickly, figuring he'd text her as soon as his meeting was over and maybe they could meet for a coffee and spend the day together. With any luck, they could pick up right where they left off.

Chapter Eleven

STELLA groaned as she started to stir. There were parts of her body that hadn't been sore in ages, but that was a good sore. The bad sore was her ankle, which hurt like a mother. Speaking of mothers, a glance at her phone revealed that her mom had tried to call her last night, right about the time that Domenico was buried deep inside her, judging by the time recorded on her phone. Ugh. She hated having to have those conversations with the woman. At least if she did it before, say, noon, her time, maybe she could get her before she was slurring her words and impossible to speak with. But after that, there was no joy in dealing with her whatsoever.

She rolled over, expecting to find Domenico there, but instead found rumpled sheets and no warm body.

Okay... Not fair, since she was the one who planned on making the break from him. But on her terms. And preferably after a pleasant little morning wake-up call. Harrumph. That did not set well with her one bit. What was he—some sort of love 'em and leave 'em type? Minus the love bit. Lust 'em and leave 'em was more appropriate. God, she hated when men pulled that crap. It was so bogus. Like somehow they were the ones who made the damned rules. *She* wanted to make the rules. *She* wanted to blow him off. *She* wanted it to be her one-night stand, dammit! Was that too much to ask?

But *dayum*. As her mind revisited what happened right here, in this very bed, seriously, could she have had the courage to ditch him? He was pretty darned good in the sack. And rather sweet. And her suspicions about what he was packing? Better than she imagined.

As much as she'd have loved to have at it one more time this morning before kicking him to the curb, in reality, he spared her the awkward au revoir moment by blowing out of there as he did while she slept. It wasn't necessarily a bad thing that he left like he did, but it made her mad that she didn't have control over the exit.

Alexa and her boyfriend, Antoine, showed their faces at around eleven as Stella's stomach started to growl. She had nothing in the apartment to eat but she was not prepared to take the four flights of steps with her ankle swollen and bruised, so she was going to make her roomie work for her betrayal.

"You had best have something super amazing to feed me," Stella said. "Because otherwise, I'm going to send you right back out to get me something. You owe me, big-time, for setting me up like you did last night."

Alexa took a look at Stella on the sofa with a bag of ice on her ankle and frowned. "What the hell is that?"

Antoine, looking perfectly French hipster with his hair in a man bun and in narrow pants, driving loafers with no socks, a white T-shirt, and a scarf wrapped around his neck, pointed at her ankle. "Did things get kinky with you and that guy, Stel? You want me to take care of him?"

Stella rolled her eyes. "I'm sure you'd pose quite the threat to Domenico, who has a good half a foot on you. And no, things did not get kinky with us."

"So what's up with that then?" Alexa said as she bent over and removed the ice to get a better look. "Hmmm… Dr. Hanigan says it looks like you have a sprain."

"Thanks for stating the obvious."

"How'd you do this? It looks sort of gnarly."

Stella waved her away. "It was a stupid tango accident."

Alexa nodded. "Of course, that explains it all. The old tango accident."

Stella waved her hand. "Stop. Can't you see I'm in pain here?"

Lexie laughed. "I was hoping you'd be suffering but more like from lovesickness."

"Oh yeah, I bet you did." Stella pouted. "You think you're some sort of magical matchmaker or something?"

"I don't know. You tell me. What happened and who'd you tango with and then I'll let you know."

Stella sighed. "Fine. Okay. So he was a nice guy. And you disappeared and those drinks were particularly yummy. Especially after the day I had. And then I decided it would be okay to throw caution to the wind and have a teensy little hookup because, well, it has been an awfully long time."

"So you decided to bring him home to tango? Sort of weird."

"No, silly. We went to the river. Where everyone goes to tango."

Antoine pointed his thumb at himself. "Wait. So I get the credit for this hookup? Sweet."

Stella squinted at him. "Not hardly. I can honestly say that thoughts of you did not cross my mind when I decided I was in the mood for a little fling."

"But the tango. I showed you that."

"You showed Lexie, and I happened to be there. But, well, yeah."

"So you were dancing and now you're maimed. We missed part of the story."

Stella shook her head. "It was super embarrassing. We were dancing. It was late and the place was packed. We were pressed up against each other—"

"Which is a good thing," Alexa said.

"But then he went one way and I went another way and I went crashing down. Needless to say, it wasn't one of my more graceful moves."

"Oh, you poor thing." Alexa shifted the bag of ice to cover the swollen part.

"But he was super chivalrous and got me back here, and he carried me all the way up the steps."

"Is he crazy?" Antoine said. "What person in their right mind would do something like that?"

Alexa swatted at him. "You, if I hurt myself. I'd make you."

They all laughed.

"So he comes back here and then what?"

"Well, normally an injury would be a bit of a buzzkill, but he was such a gentleman, and like I said, it had been a long time and, well, you weren't here."

"Ewww, I'm going to change the sheets right now." Alexa held her nose in jest.

"Already done," Stella said.

"Omigod, so you slept with him? On the first date?"

Stella smiled. "It wasn't even a date. I think it totally qualifies as a hookup, right? I'm pretty proud of myself that I simply pulled the trigger and did it."

"And so you're seeing each other later?"

Stella frowned. "Hell no. I didn't say I was dating the man. I said I was having a fling. I had the fling, it's done. We have our class starting tomorrow, and I won't have time for that nonsense. Besides, he's only visiting. He'll be leaving probably by tomorrow, who knows? I don't have to worry about that stuff. It was a lot of fun, but I don't have time for men in my life. Besides, men leave. I'm never going to give one a chance to leave me—I'll always be the first one out the door."

"Stella, you are a hopeless romantic," Antoine said as he reached for his girlfriend's hand and kissed his way up her arm.

"Right?" Alexa said. "I mean you have this guy, who is clearly interested in you, and you're not going to give it a chance?"

"I'll leave the charming romance to you two lovebirds. Meantime I need you to feed me something good to make up for selling me out to the easiest hookup. Get cooking." She clapped her hands as the two of them laughed at her.

"Mark my words, Stella Whitaker. You're going to regret it if you don't follow up with him. Domenico Romeo is the real deal."

Stella plugged her ears and whistled. She was afraid the more she thought about Domenico Romeo, the more she might realize her friend was right.

Chapter Twelve

DOMENICO had sent five texts over the past two hours to Stella and she didn't reply to a single one of them. Which sucked. He could tell she was like one of those cats you reach your hand out to pet and it comes that close to you then runs scared behind the bushes. There was no reasoning with a timid cat. But damn, as timid as she seemed to be about men—or was it only him—she was certainly not timid when it came to sex. That woman was in it to win it, and despite her injured ankle, she came, she saw, and she conquered. Not necessarily in that order.

Yet as much fun as they had in bed together, he probably enjoyed dancing and chatting with her even more. She was fun and interesting. And if he was to be completely honest, a little bit challenging. And he always loved to rise to a challenge. For that matter, coming to Paris, deciding to take the step he was about to take, was indicative of that. Clearly he needed to shake things up, be it in his personal or professional life, so maybe the universe had sent the obstinate Stella Whitaker his way to make it that much harder.

And to the universe, he had one thing to say: Bring. It.

Domenico stopped for a croissant and a cappuccino—he was, after all, Italian, and couldn't go without his breakfast coffee drink—on his way to his first day of class. It felt weird to be going back to school again. Not like this was your conventional kind of school, but maybe it would lead to him to take the plunge and go all in with the culinary end of things.

For now, merely attending the intensive wine course at l'école Marondi was going to be a huge leap. He hadn't told his family what he was doing. Instead he'd said he wanted a break so decided to take a little getaway to Paris. They didn't need to know what he was doing there; it was a big deal simply for him to assert his independence this much in a family that expected everyone to toe the family line.

As he approached the wide granite staircase of the school, with students milling about finishing their coffees and chatting, he took a deep breath. It was going to be weird, being this man who'd been out in the world, active in his business, all of a sudden a mere student again. Weirder still since here he knew so much about his wine, but now he was going to have to learn about French wine, and well, everyone knew the French thought they invented wine. He laughed at his little joke. After all, everyone knew the Italians invented it. Or at least the good stuff.

He walked past the thicket of students milling about on the sidewalk and entered through the tall oak doors and into the large hallway where he'd been for meetings only the day before. He'd had to talk the school's director into letting him in without going through the proper admissions channels—normally you couldn't just show up for one class but rather had to be an enrolled student. Thank goodness Romeo wines were known the world over. After discussion amongst senior staff at the school, they decided to allow Domenico to attend the two-week intensive course with no obligation to continue with any other classes. It would be his little secret that he was entertaining the idea of doing that.

He walked the length of the lobby and took the stairs to the basement, where he was greeted with the strong smell of alcohol looming in the air. The familiar aroma of many bottles of wine breathing in the classroom wafted outward through the doorway.

He entered and took a seat in the front row. He didn't want to be the teacher's pet but he did want to absorb as much as possible, and if that meant sitting front and center he would. He looked at his watch: a good fifteen minutes until the class would start. He opened up an app on his phone for the *Corriere della Sera* newspaper, content to catch up on what was going on in his country while he waited for class to begin.

Soon students began filtering into the classroom. He wanted to be inconspicuous, but occasionally he lifted his head to see who arrived. About a minute before class was scheduled to start, he heard her voice.

"I am so sitting in the back of the classroom," he heard Stella say. "I hate wine. It tastes like medicine to me. I'm only taking this course because I was told it was essential before leaving the school."

He turned around and noticed there wasn't a remaining place to sit in the back of the room. Instead, the only two seats left were in the front—one to Domenico's right, and the other to his left. Alexa was the first to seat herself, and upon noticing Domenico, waved hello as the instructor arrived.

Hobbling in behind the teacher was Stella, garbed in the traditional toque hat and chef's coat, with her name embroidered on it. He was so impressed with her professional appearance. He was not invited to dress as the students did since he wasn't officially enrolled at l'école Marondi, which made him feel a bit wistful. But more immediately, he felt terrible about her ankle, which was obviously bothering her. He stood to help her to her seat, but she grimaced at him and shook off his offer of assistance.

As soon as she sat down, she turned her back to Domenico, making it clear she was going to have nothing to do with him.

Okay, then. She wanted to play hard to get? He'd dealt with worse in his life.

The instructor introduced himself as Monsieur Gabonarde and offered a brief overview of what the class would focus on.

"Normally I focus purely on French wines, because, well, after all, this is France. However we have a guest in our midst with a deep knowledge of Italian wines, Chianti, in particular, so we'll pay some attention to the wines of this region as well, to at least expose you to alternatives to the wines of my country. Which I would argue are far superior." He nodded and gave a friendly wink to Domenico, who smiled.

"But first, we will begin with champagne, the world's most famous sparkling wine."

Glasses of champagne were passed around as Monsieur Gabonarde described the second fermentation in the bottle, the half turns the winemaker makes to ensure proper fermentation, and discussed the three grapes used for champagne: Chardonnay, Pinot Noir, and Pinot Meunier.

"You use all of your senses when you are tasting wine. *Dégustation* means tasting, *la robe* is the look of the wine, *le nez* is the smell, right? From the French word for 'nose.' *Le gout* is the flavor, the taste."

He held up the straw-colored champagne, swirling it gently in his glass. "There are many flavors you will discern as you go through the step-by-step process of exploring each wine. You might notice a grassiness, perhaps a citrus-like undertone. There could be fruit, perhaps apple. Maybe the slightest hint of strawberry. Pay attention to these flavors, and as the champagne rolls on your tongue, you'll pick up deeper flavor notes. Some of these will have layers of different flavors. It is the joy of wine."

Domenico glanced over at Stella, who looked like she'd just sucked on a lemon. He frowned.

"You don't like it?"

She pursed her lips. "I hate champagne. For that matter, I don't like wine. I don't understand how people like it. Give me a good mixed drink any day over this swill."

"Swill?" One thing Domenico didn't like was someone insulting a perfectly good wine.

"Perhaps you've not had the right wine to appeal to your fickle palate. To reject wine would be akin to rejecting mother's milk."

"I was bottle-fed."

"That was a euphemism." He frowned. "You must like some sort of wine. Have you ever tried a Super Tuscan?" He didn't dare suggest his own family's wine; she'd probably throw her champagne glass at him.

She shook her head vehemently. "Nope. I think wine sucks."

"Then why are you in a wine class?"

"I think the better question is why are you in a wine class, Mr. Oenophile? Are you stalking me or something? Because honestly it doesn't thrill me that you just showed up here."

Domenico knit his brow. *Mr. Oenophile?* He wondered what had gotten her panties in such a wad.

"I didn't know you were going to be in this class when I registered—I didn't know you existed at the time! I signed up for this completely independently of you. And quite frankly, how would I have known you would be here if I did know of you then? You failed to respond to any of my voice mail or text messages. For all I know you were trapped in your apartment, unable to walk for the past several days, starving to death."

"Thanks for your concern for my welfare."

"One can only attempt to communicate so much before it becomes a moot point."

She rolled her eyes. "Look, Domenico. I appreciate your help the other night, and yeah, we had a fun little time of it. But I'm not looking for something with a guy, especially one I'm never going to see again after a few days. To be truthful, if I'd have known you were going to be in this class, I'd have never let things get so out of hand. I hope you'll understand."

I hope you'll understand. If she was going for clichéd brush-offs, he'd have rather she said, "It's not you, it's me."

But if she'd rather blow off a good man who was interested in her, well, that was her choice. There were plenty of women knocking at his door. He didn't need to beg.

Except something inside him kind of wanted to beg for her. Desperately.

Chapter Thirteen

STELLA was ready to hurl her phone against the wall. She was now into the double digits for number of phone calls trying to track down her missing carry-on bag, which was still nowhere to be found.

"This is starting to tick me off." She made a growling sound.

"Starting to?" Alexa lifted an eyebrow.

"Okay, fine, it's making me angrier. I was already ticked off."

"Much better," Alexa said. "At least you're not blaming that sweet Domenico guy."

Stella stared at her through slitted eyelids. "I thought I made it clear that I don't want to talk about him."

"I know you said that. But a) I don't understand it and b) I think deep down you don't mean it."

"That's ridiculous." Stella threw her arms up in the air. "What's not to understand?"

Alexa held up her pointer finger, beginning to enumerate. "Um, first off, he likes you. Second, you like him. Third, he's a sweet guy. Fourth, he's got a rockin' body. Fifth, he has this interesting family history that would be so fun to explore. Sixth—"

Stella shook her head. "I feel like I'm watching a counting segment on *Sesame Street*. Enough with your 'hundred reasons why Stella should marry Domenico' debate."

"I didn't say marry the guy," Alexa said. "I only mean give him a chance."

"I gave him a chance!"

"I didn't say bang him till dawn, Stel. By give him a chance, I mean maybe you could go on another date."

"That would mean I've already been on a date with him. Which I haven't, thanks."

"You had drinks, you went dancing—"

"Let me clarify: you and I went for drinks where one or both of you bombshelled me with his presence."

"Bombshelled?"

"Sorry, couldn't think of a better term. But you know what I mean. The last person on the planet I wanted or needed to see was that Romeo man."

"I could argue, judging by how the evening turned out, that he was precisely the right person on the planet for you."

Stella was going to get a headache from rolling her eyes so much. "Come off it, Lex. A hookup doesn't mean it was a match made in heaven. It means I was horny, he was horny, and I needed help getting up the stairs."

Lexie smiled. "I know one thing that didn't need any help getting up."

"Stop!" Stella swatted at her friend. "Go away. I don't want to talk about this."

"Which is precisely why we're talking about this."

"About what?"

"About your habit of self-sabotage in relationships."

"I didn't know I was rooming with Oprah."

"I'm serious. You know that you avoid anything that slightly smacks of having to open yourself up to a man."

"Besides, with Domenico, we just had a thing."

"By 'thing' you mean you got scared because relationships require, well, relating? And you don't want to find yourself in the position of having to do that with a man?"

Stella put her fingertip up to the tip of her nose. "Ding. Ding. Ding. Give the girl a cookie."

"And they thought armchair psychology was a challenge." Alexa puffed some air on her nails then buffed them against her chest. "Who needs advanced degrees in clinical psychology? Stick with me and I can figure out all your emotional baggage in ten easy sessions." She laughed, but Stella simply frowned at her.

"It's not a big deal. Besides, as long as things are good in bed, that's all that matters."

"I think what matters is that you need to open up to a man you're with."

"I'd say I opened up to him quite willingly." She covered her mouth with her hand, surprised she actually said that.

"I don't mean sexually," Alexa said. "That's easy. It's much easier to sleep with someone you hardly know than to forge a bond and truly expose yourself emotionally."

"Ugh," Stella said. "Emotions are so messy. Who needs 'em?"

"Says the woman who needs them the most but doesn't recognize it. And instead chooses to suppress them." She placed her hands on her friend's shoulders and looked hard into her eyes. "Look, Stel, you know I'm only saying this because I care about you, don't you?"

Stella glanced away, hating to hear the truth. "You just like to be a matchmaker."

"I could care less about being a matchmaker. In fact it's a real pain in the ass if whatever little I've done with you and Domenico is any bellwether. Trust me, there are easier lines of work. Like being a chef."

They both laughed at that, knowing as they did what a tough profession it was, for women in particular. Working in the culinary arts meant long hours on your feet, an aching back, and rough behavior from some in the kitchen. Often women had to outperform men tenfold to be accepted.

"You might have noticed I plan to go out on my own professionally as well," Stella said. "I don't like to be beholden to others. I like to rely on me. I know I can rely on me."

Alexa pressed the heel of her hand to her forehead. "But there are lots of people rooting for you. People you can and should rely upon. We're there for that very reason. We're not going to abandon you like your folks did, metaphorically or literally. Can't you see that?"

Stella shook her head. "Maybe I happen to prefer my brand of severe independence."

Her friend laughed. "Severe independence. Right." She shook her head. "I'm telling you, that's gonna be boring if for no other reason then you'll not have great sex."

Stella threw her shade, giving Lexie her best "you're crazy, lady" look. "Uh, I had fabulous sex with Domenico several nights ago. Great sex and being stuck in a relationship do not have to go hand in hand."

"Stuck in a relationship? Is that how you view it? Stuck?"

Stella nodded. "Well, of course I do. You're trapped with someone else telling you how to live your life and what to do and when to eat and all that stuff. No, thank you, ma'am."

"Are you telling me you've never been in a nurturing relationship with a man?"

Stella pursed her lips in thought. "Well, I had a super nice history teacher in sixth grade. Mr. Rutherford. I'd sometimes sit in his room and talk with him when my mom forgot to pick me up after school." She grinned.

Alexa laughed and thumped her friend playfully on the head. "You are such a weirdo. And I'm sorry your mom forgot to pick you up. You know that's her, not you, don't you?"

Stella nodded. "Intellectually, yes. But emotionally? It feels pretty shitty when your father leaves, your mother drinks and no-shows half the time, and your stepmother simply wants you to disappear."

"You definitely got a raw deal, no question about it. But it doesn't mean your whole life has to be about rejection. Especially considering you've now flipped the table and reject men before—"

"Before they have a chance to reject me. I know, I know."

"So you seriously haven't ever been in a healthy relationship with a man?"

"Honey I haven't been in a healthy relationship with anyone. Ever. Lest you forget from whence I sprang. Girlfriend, I was raised by wolves."

Alexa wagged her finger at her friend. "I can tell you one healthy relationship you've had."

"Oh, this should be rich."

She turned her finger to point at her chest. "Um, yours truly."

Stella winced. "Awww, Lex. I didn't mean to exclude you." She reached out to give her a hug. "Of course you're my good friend. And I appreciate that. I do consider you my best friend. You know that. But I don't think I'm capable of being in anything more than a fleeting 'thing' with a guy. It's not part of my DNA."

"I don't believe that the inability to commit is a genetic thing. I think it's all up here." She pointed to her head. "And it comes down to choices. You can choose whether you're going to let the terrorists win. And by terrorists, I mean all the baggage that haunts you—you don't want to let it go."

The buzzer rang from someone outside.

Alexa pressed the intercom button.

"I have a package here for Stella Whitaker."

"I'll buzz you up. We're on the fourth floor." She turned to her roommate. "You expecting something?"

"Not a thing. I'm only glad it's not Domenico coming to woo me."

Alexa shook her head. "You're insufferable, woman. For the record, I think you're making a big mistake. He's one of the good guys. It will be your loss if you let that slip away for lack of trying on your part."

"No such thing as a good guy. There are only guys. Period."

Alexa started to say something but refrained.

There was a knock on the door and Stella hobbled over to open it.

The delivery person handed her an exquisite hot pink Tumi suitcase with an oversized bright yellow bow.

"What the hell?"

He handed her an envelope and stood there. She took the hint and pulled a couple of euros from her purse and tipped him.

She ran her fingers beneath the edge of the envelope and slipped a note from it.

I figured you could never lose a bag this bright," the note said. *"Not that I am admitting guilt by association, but rather I am disassociating myself by simply replacing these. I couldn't sleep at night knowing the Leonardo of the cake world would be without her essential tools. But seriously, I'm sorry for whatever role I inadvertently had in the loss of the first one. I hope you'll find the replacements to your satisfaction. Maybe if I'm lucky someday, you'll use them for a cake for me.*

Stella felt a little sick to her stomach.

"What?" Alexa said. "You look like someone just kicked your dog."

Stella shook her head to refocus. "Oh. Hmmm. I'm sorry. I don't know why."

Alexa pointed to the suitcase. "So what's up with that?"

"It's from Domenico. He sent this as a replacement for my lost bag and all my baking supplies." She looked up at her roommate. "But how would he know what was in that suitcase?"

Alexa, averted her gaze, pretending to distract herself by whistling.

"You colluded with him to do this?" Stella said, frowning.

Alexa held up her hands. "I didn't collude with him! He asked me what was in there and I told him. He wanted to make things whole again."

"But, Lex, this makes things so damned complicated."

"Yeah. Sure. Complicated." Alexa knit her brow. "You lost all your supplies. They cost a fortune. You don't have the money to replace them. And he kindly does so for you. I totally get it. That's super complicated."

Stella stuck her tongue out at Alexa, then rolled the suitcase toward the sofa and sat down, opening the thing up. "It does because now how can I simply ignore him and pretend he's not there when I go to class tomorrow?" She started sifting through the stockpile of supplies, checking to see if there was anything missing. The knives—from the bread knife to the chef's to the paring and cake slicing, even the sharpening steel—were all a better brand than the ones she'd purchased. Spatulas, scrapers, a digital thermometer, whisks, top-of-the-line kitchen shears, decorating tips, the list went on and on. He didn't miss one thing.

Her hands shook as she sorted through it all. "I don't know what to say."

Lexie held up her finger as if she'd just invented the light bulb. "I've got a brilliant idea. Why don't you pick up the phone and call him? You could go out on a limb and thank the man."

"Crap, you don't understand," Stella said as she burst into tears, stood, and ran from the room.

Chapter Fourteen

DOMENICO was in his hotel catching up on emails when he received a phone call from Alexa.

"So? How'd it go?" he said, a tinge of hope in his voice. He looked out his window at the water of the Seine reflecting the late-day sun, thinking he'd go for a run. He needed some time to chill.

He heard a tsking sound, which didn't bode well.

"I'm sorry, Domenico." Alexa sighed. "I'm afraid it's complicated. Stella's a sweetheart, truly she is. But she's been so damaged by how she was raised, I think she's super scared."

Domenico drummed his fingers on the desk as he stared out at the view of the magnificent cathedral of Notre-Dame in the distance. "I guess it's a no-go then? I mean I'd like to take a chance to get to know her better, but I'm also not a glutton for punishment. It kind of feels like the universe is trying to tell me something here."

"The universe has got nothing to do with this," she said. "This is simply Stella being a stinker. Listen, I honestly think you two have got something. You both have that combustible feeling you get right before a storm blows in. I hope you won't give up quite yet. You might be the catalyst for change that Stella has needed in her life for a long, long time."

"How very romantic, being a chemical reaction."

"Sometimes to get to the romance you have to have a breakthrough."

"More like a chisel and hammer."

"I'm not gonna lie. This is going to be harder than I expected. But I have an idea."

"Please, don't tell me it involves springing me on her unexpectedly. So far that hasn't been too well received."

"I would argue that it worked pretty successfully the first time. Perhaps too much and she ran scared. I've never seen her react that badly. It's like you bring out the worst in her. In a good way."

He nodded. "Gee, thanks. I think." He let out a big sigh. "I mean, yeah. Ultimately, things turned out well that night. But obviously it ended up backfiring. Which would be fine if I was looking for a one-night stand. And it would describe most men on the planet. But for some reason, I'd like to explore the idea of more with Stella. God knows why." He chuckled.

"So then let's make it happen."

"Good luck with that."

"Do you ride bikes?"

"Yeah, sure, I can ride a bike."

"In that case, I'm cooking an idea."

"I hope you're as good a cook with schemes as you are in a kitchen—which I assume you are since you're almost done with culinary school."

"Correction: pastry school. Though I am a kick-ass chef, period."

"And this scheme you're devising?"

"Paris has the best network of bike shares. The first thirty minutes are free, which is amazing. You can ride all day. All you have to do is swap out bikes at a bike station every half hour and you never have to pay! You can keep going like that all day long."

"I said I can ride a bike, but I can't navigate a bike alone in Paris without ending up as roadkill. And honestly, the money doesn't matter. I'm fine paying my way."

"It's okay. Hear me out," Alexa said. "The 'biking in Paris' bit is where Antoine comes into play. He's a native Parisian, and he's been riding and roaming the streets of this city his whole life. I'm going to have him take you out, show you the ropes so you can figure out how to borrow the bikes, and then we're all going to conveniently meet up at one of the bike stations and voila, we'll all go off together and picnic somewhere. It'll be good because although she'll know it was a setup, she'll at least stick around. Then we all hang out together for a while, and you surprise her with something amazing and we'll leave you two to have fun."

"Surprise her with something amazing in Paris? Like, oh, I reserve the Eiffel Tower for her privately?" he laughed.

"Don't be silly. There are lots of things you can do that will impress a poor culinary school student. Like how about an intimate boat ride along the Seine? She'd love that."

Domenico thought about that. "You think she'd actually go with me?"

"I'll guilt her into it if she balks."

"Exactly what I want—a guilt-driven date."

"Like I said, this is going to take some monumental effort. But I do think if you use that hammer and chisel, eventually you're going to find a beautiful statue emerging."

"One made of stone."

"Let's not get ahead of ourselves and worry about that yet."

He kicked his legs up on top of the desk and leaned back, contemplating. This plan sounded like it was ripe for failure, but shy of an alternative, what did he have to lose?

"I guess, what could go wrong?" But as he expressed that thought out loud, he couldn't help but feel like only about ten thousand things could fall apart with this tightly woven plan. For some bizarre reason, though, he was game for giving it a try.

Chapter Fifteen

STELLA and Alexa sat outside at their favorite patisserie, sipping cappuccinos and enjoying brioche.

"It's going to be a gorgeous day. I'd love to ride bikes. We could get supplies for a picnic and chill out for the afternoon. You up for that?"

Stella nodded. "I'd be down with that. Just you and me, or is loverboy joining us?"

Alexa flicked her on the arm. "Ha ha. You're jealous."

"Yeah the day I'm jealous of someone stuck with a boyfriend is the day you need to check the weather to see if hell has frozen over." She stirred some sugar into her cappuccino.

Alexa laughed. "You have such a colorful way of putting things. But I still think that if given the right set of circumstances, you could find happiness with a man."

Stella pretended to pull her hair out. "You are so starting to sound like a broken record."

"Although neither of us actually knows what a broken record sounds like." Alexa winked at her. "But I would argue that you're the broken record, sistah."

"How so?"

"In your dogged determination to not allow things to unfold with that sweet Domenico."

"Oh, so now he's that sweet Domenico? You do know I'm struggling not to roll my eyes nonstop here."

"Well, he is sweet. And he's thoughtful. Not to dredge up bad memories or anything, but he bought you a gorgeous four-hundred-dollar suitcase and filled it with another five-hundred-dollars' worth of supplies. I know that was super shitty of him to do and that alone is reason to avoid him at all costs..."

Stella flipped her friend the finger. "You know I can't go there."

"Oooh, yeah. Do I ever. But I've been thinking more about this—"

"Nothing good will come of that, you know."

"Fine, Stella. I get it. You think you're not interested in the sweet, kind, thoughtful, tango-dancing, luggage-replacing Italian man. But hear me out. Consider this. You had this hookup with the guy, right?"

"Don't remind me." Although as soon as the words came out of her mouth Stella knew she was full of shit. Make that *merde*, since, after all, she was in France. Her mind had been busy reminding her practically nonstop about what it felt like to have his hard, naked body pressed to hers, his mouth over her lips, his hands roaming her body, his entire being shuddering alongside hers. She was going to be in deep trouble if she wasn't careful.

"Now, stop, and let me talk for a minute without any of that Negative Nancy stuff, okay? Like I said, you hooked up with Domenico. And normally, that's exactly what a guy's after—a hookup. He's perfectly happy to get the hell out of dodge and never see the woman again. But yet here's Domenico, who is so sweet, he actually wants to spend time with you. Maybe not even in bed. But, like, *with* you.

Yet you're practically lobbing hand grenades at him. I don't see why you can't try a new tack. I mean, nothing personal, but obviously whatever you've been doing isn't working so well."

"Why do I get the feeling this is a prelude to some sort of setup?"

Alexa lifted her eyebrow and smiled. "Would I do something like that?"

"Would you? You already did!"

"I'm not going to say anything else except this: trust in the universe."

"Oh, now you're gonna go all woo-woo on me? Are you going to whip out your crystals and dab some patchouli oil on and maybe light an incense stick?"

Alexa shook her head. "Very funny. No, I am simply telling you to take a deep breath, stop overthinking everything, and maybe for once, go with the bloody damned flow. Now, let me text Antoine and we'll plan to meet him midafternoon for our picnic."

"As long as you know I'm totally onto you, my friend. The only reason I'm going willingly right now is I know you haven't had time to track down Domenico and loop him in on this. But as soon as I feel it's not safe to go in the water, if I see the shark fins on the horizon, I'm gonna retreat to the safety of the shoreline. You got it?"

"Trust me, I have been schooled." And Stella wondered if she should trust the grin that broke out across her good friend's face.

As the two women made their way along the streets of Paris, they stopped at their favorite local shops to collect the supplies for their picnic: they picked up their *tradition*, or baguettes, at a boulangerie in the Marais and cheeses from a *fromagerie* in the ninth arrondissement. They couldn't agree on where to buy pastries, so they went to two places: first to Laurent Favre-Mot Pâtisserie, where Paris's most famous TV celebrity chef created such playful desserts as his renowned "Fucking Dark Chocolate," made up of a chocolate cookie slathered with chocolate ganache, topped with milk chocolate Chantilly, a chocolate tile, and capped off with a sweet chocolate skull. Stella loved the irreverence of the rogue, bearded, tattooed hipster pastry chef who sported a Mickey Mouse tat on his neck.

Alexa preferred traditional French pastries so opted to stop at *confiseur* and pâtissier Sebastien Gaudard's shop for *mussipontaine*, which he made in homage to his pastry chef father. The soft and crunchy, sweet and savory concoction consisted of meringue made with almond powder, filled with vanilla cream and edged with caramelized almonds.

"I'm sorry but I don't think I can wait till later to eat this," Alexa said. "Any chance you'll split one with me now?"

Stella laughed. "Did you actually have to ask such a ridiculous question?"

Alexa pulled out her Opinel knife, which no self-respecting Parisian would be without, and sliced the pastry in half.

Stella took a bite, and her eyes rolled back in her head. "Oh. My. God." She moaned. "Why have I never had this before?"

"Right? I've been telling you about this for ages. This is, hands down, the best pastry on the planet."

"Oh, best pastry doesn't do it justice. This is downright orgasmic. I mean actually better than sex."

Alexa wiped some pastry cream from her lips. "How about a close second. I mean, I bet you it wasn't better than sex with Domenico."

Stella shook her head. "You don't let up, do you?"

"I'm only saying, you yourself told me it was pretty fabulous."

Stella popped the rest of the pastry into her mouth and chewed while she contemplated. "Honestly it's hard to say. I mean this is pretty absolutely perfect. But then again, when it all happened, so was that."

"Well, then, I guess it's good you don't have to decide one over the other. You can have your cake and have sex with Domenico too." She gave Stella a friendly little push on the shoulder, and Stella gave her a tepid smile.

"Enough of this talk of men who are not in my life," Stella said. "We'd better get a move on if we're going to get to the park in time to meet up with loverboy."

"Speaking of, I think my text dinged, so let me check to see if that's Antoine." She pulled out her phone. "Oh, cool. He said he has a great place for us to stop at before we go to our picnic—he said to meet at the *Institut du Monde Arabe*. The Arab World Institute."

"Huh. I wonder what's there?"

"I don't know but I guess we'll see. Sounds like a good surprise."

Sophie winced. She was so not a fan of surprises.

Chapter Sixteen

IT'S always best when a local shows you places off the beaten path, and Antoine was no exception. He took Domenico through areas the average tourist would never see and the two had fun riding through Paris. They'd gone to a market and purchased some locally made charcuterie, and they found a wine shop that Domenico wanted to go to—he knew they would carry the Romeo wine he was looking for.

Their next stop was to meet up with the girls for a special diversion before the picnic. He wasn't sure what to expect or if Stella would simply whack him over the head with a baguette and pedal away.

They returned their bikes to a nearby station and walked across a plaza to the entrance of the Arab World Institute. When Domenico turned to look for Stella and Alexa, they approached, each with shopping totes over their shoulders. He took a deep breath, bracing himself for the onslaught.

"Ahhh… Domenico! *Quelle surprise!*" Alexa said. *What a surprise!*

Stella knit her brow. "Quelle surprise, indeed," she said in what sounded to Domenico like a mutter.

Alexa leaned in to offer her cheek in the traditional *faire la bise*, the two-cheek kiss with which the French greet one another. Domenico returned the courtesy, and Alexa turned her attention to Antoine, leaving Domenico to fend for himself with—or against—Stella.

"So, we meet again," she said.

"Yes, it seems we've got to stop meeting like this." He leaned over to faire la bise, and she obliged him, just barely. If he had to bet money, he'd wager she'd rather have dental surgery than allow him to touch her cheek with his.

"Gee, ya think?"

They stood together in awkward silence for probably thirty seconds before Antoine mercifully interrupted them.

"Follow me—we'll take the elevator up to the rooftop."

"The rooftop?" Stella said. "I didn't know they had one you could go on."

"Every now and again, if you're lucky, you can get access to the top of this amazing building and enjoy a whole different glimpse of the Parisian skyline. Today, it seems, is your lucky day."

They entered through the main doors of the beautifully designed contemporary-yet-Moorish-influenced glassed building and rode the elevator to the top floor. They came out onto a large rooftop area with a restaurant to one side and a stunning 360-degree view of Paris.

"This view of my city rivals that which you'd see from the top of *la tour Eiffel*," Antoine said, his arms extended and sweeping across the horizon.

"You can't exactly miss Notre-Dame, can you?" Stella said, pointing at the beautiful cathedral on the famed Île de la Cité, the small island in the middle of the Seine River. It seemed so close you could almost touch it. She pointed farther to the left. "Over there is the stunning Sainte-Chapelle—a Gothic chapel with the most magnificent stained glass windows. You can attend concerts there almost nightly."

"I'd love to do that," Domenico said, seizing on the fact she was willing to actually speak to him. "Maybe you could take me?" He held up his hands in surrender. "As friends, of course."

"I think that would be a lovely idea," Alexa said, locking arms with Stella. "A little culture, a little international camaraderie, sounds like the makings of a fairy tale, uh, er, friendship." She gave Domenico a wink and elbowed Stella.

"With friends like you… I might want to consider new friends."

"Awww, come on, you love me, admit it." Alexa squeezed her friend's cheeks and puckered up for a kiss. "I absolutely love that you found this secret view for us, sweetie," she said, turning to Antoine. "I wish we could stay up here to eat. And my stomach is demanding pastries, so who's in favor of our picnic?"

All hands shot up, so the group headed toward the elevator, found a bike-share station, and hopped on bikes for the short ride to the Jardin du Luxembourg, a sprawling public garden in Saint Germain-des-Prés.

"Funny how all roads lead us back to where you live," Domenico said, trying to make small talk.

"You mean the scene of the crime?" Alexa looked back at the two of them and winked.

Alexa was sure laying it on think. Domenico hoped she knew what she was doing.

They parked their bikes at the nearest station and walked the rest of the way, entering through the tall gates into the exquisitely laid-out gardens.

They entered the pebbled pathways and walked along tree-lined promenades edged by brilliant beds of purple, yellow, and blue flowers, in the direction of the magnificent Palais du Luxembourg, once the residence of Marie de' Medici, the mother of Louis XIII. In front of them was a large circular pond where children operated remote control sailboats.

"Welcome to Luxembourg Gardens," Alexa said, her arms outspread. "Fun fact, it was modeled on the Boboli Gardens in Florence, which I hear are totally stunning."

"Ahhh… *Giardino di Boboli*," Domenico said. "I've been there many a time. Part of the *Palazzo Pitti*, the Pitti Palace. It's the place that reinforced to me that the Medici family were the original hoarders."

"Seriously?" Stella said.

"I mean I don't think they had a clinical psychiatric diagnosis, per se, but if you go into that palace, there is barely a space that isn't taken up with 'stuff.' And by stuff, I mean priceless works of art, stunning antiques, and ancient rugs and tapestries and jewelry and silver and bone china. Honestly one day wandering through that place and you feel as if your head will explode from the excess of it all."

"Quite the ringing endorsement." Stella laughed.

"Don't get me wrong—the grandeur is off the charts. The place is truly something to behold. But it's just so much, it's hard to ingest it all at once. But the gardens— that's one of my favorite places to go in Florence. They're vast and varied and sprawling and comfortable and the views of the city are wonderful. Maybe someday I can take you there."

He knew it was a huge gamble for him to dare suggest something so intimate as them traveling somewhere together. Not like they hadn't already been intimate, but that was different. He could tell by the way she'd treated him. To her, that was a one-off. Sure, maybe it was a little too close for her and—as if burned by touching a flame—she had to jump back from it for her own self-protection. But the fact was, he loved the Boboli Gardens. He'd attended weddings and special events there and had spent many an afternoon relaxing beneath the generous shade of a sycamore tree with the palace before him and the famed Brunelleschi's Dome in the distance.

He worried that now was the time she might pull out that baguette and choke up on it like a baseball bat and lob him hard.

Stella looked at him, a serious look on her face. "Huh," she said. "That might be something fun to do."

Chapter Seventeen

THAT *might be something fun to do*. Fun to do? What the hell was she saying? For that matter, what the hell was she thinking? Who had taken temporary occupancy of her brain and spoken those betraying words? And how exactly could she backpedal on that response without coming across like a complete jerk? Ugh. Maybe he hadn't noticed. Maybe no one heard her. That would be perfect. She hadn't said it all that loudly. Cool. More than likely it would remain her secret forever.

"I'm sorry, what did you say?" Domenico said, his brow knit.

"She said she'd love to go there with you," Alexa said, chucking her friend on the arm.

Stella's eyes opened wide and she tried to communicate through them that she was ready to throttle Alexa for that.

"Maybe we could make a weekend of it—Antoine and I would love to go to Florence for fun," Alexa said. "After all, when we were there last week it was all work, wasn't it, Stella?"

Sella continued to stare at her, hoping that some sort of osmosis or transmogrification or one of those processes would magically cause this entire conversation to reverse by about three minutes so she could start again with what she truly wanted to say: it would be a grave mistake for her to lead Domenico on, she didn't have it in her to deal with relationships even if he was a nice guy and everyone was right that he was worth giving it a go with, and yeah, she had been sort of a bitch to him but she didn't mean to be—it was her way of taking care to not get hurt.

But then she realized that what she wanted to say was probably exactly what she did say: it might be fun to go there with him. They had a lovely evening together at Prescription and then dancing. And he carried her up four flights of steps, for God's sake. The man should get bonus points for that. A medal even.

She kind of shook her shoulders loose a little, thrusting them back, then unclenched her fists, which she'd noticed had been in tight balls. Okay, so she hadn't bought a plane ticket and they weren't actually going there. She said it could be fun. And it could be fun. So she wasn't signing a blood oath. There would be no immediate handing over of first-born children involved. She didn't even have a first-born child to sacrifice to the cause. She could do this. She could have a perfectly pleasant and civil conversation with this man, who had been nothing but nice to her (well, except for that whole flight thing—she still wasn't ready to let bygones be bygones with that whole thing although she knew deep down how ridiculous that was).

"So, who's ready for some food?" Stella said, removing her tote bag from her shoulder and pulling out a sheet she'd tucked in for the picnic. She grabbed two ends and flapped it in the wind to try to lay it flat and Domenico moved over to hold on to the opposing ends to help. Once the blanket was spread out on the ground, the two couples sat on it—Domenico much too close for comfort—and Stella and Alexa started setting out food from their bags.

Alexa leaned over. "Way to go, Stel," she said in a whisper. "I'm so proud of you."

Stella took a deep breath. "I don't want to talk about it. Do you want some cheese?" She half shoved the bag of cheese at her friend.

She was clearly in change-the-subject mode today and it seemed to be working for her.

Domenico, meantime, was busy pulling the cork from a bottle of wine and poured and passed glasses to each of them.

"I know you don't care for wine," he said to Stella. "But I thought perhaps you hadn't had the right wine yet. If you do like it, there's plenty more where this comes from."

Antoine held the bottle up to read it. "What's this go for, per bottle? Maybe two hundred euro?"

Stella's eyes got wide yet again. This day was quite full of surprises.

"You probably don't want to know," Domenico said.

People paid like hundreds of dollars for something they were going to drink then pee out in a matter of hours? She was definitely not living in that stratosphere. Hell, she was throwing caution to the wind when she ponied up more than about twelve euro for a bottle. Which wasn't much since she usually paid far more for expensive mixed drinks. Which didn't make a whole lot of sense, did it?

"Wow, Domenico, you didn't have to spend all this for us." Alexa held her glass up to inspect it in the sunlight. "But I'm glad you did." She giggled.

"I'm happy to be able to share the fruits of my family's labor, quite literally," he said. "I appreciate your hospitality as I've become acquainted with the city. It's a little strange. I feel as if I've run away from home. But you've sort of taken me in and helped me to feel welcome." He held up his glass to theirs. "This could probably breathe a little bit more but under the circumstances, I say let's drink it. Salute." He nodded toward Stella first, and then the others.

They all tapped glasses and proceeded to take their first sip. Domenico watched Stella as she brought the glass to her lips, and she could sense his eyes on her. But it didn't seem creepy. Well, maybe it put her a teensy bit on-the-spot, but it was kind of okay. Ish.

He tipped his head forward, lifting his eyebrows, his glance hopeful. "Well?"

She looked at everyone watching her and waited a minute. "So maybe this wine-tasting class is having an effect on me, because, well, I actually like this stuff." She took another sip to be sure and nodded.

Domenico smiled. "I'm so happy you liked it. I've never met a soul who hated our wine, so it would have been a first."

She shrugged. "I'm grateful you didn't put that pressure on me before I tried it or I'd have lied to you."

"Be honest, Stel. You'd more than likely have dumped it on his head." Alexa winked at her.

"Thanks for the vote of confidence. But yeah, you might be right about that." She was willing to poke a little fun at herself. Under the right circumstances. She looked skyward, wondering if perhaps the moon and stars were in proper alignment because frankly, this was all new to her and she needed some explanation.

The four friends broke bread and shared the cheeses and the selection of cured meats the guys had purchased at the street market. Then they divvied up the desserts so each of them had a chance to taste both treats.

"I feel like I ate a giraffe," Alexa said, rubbing her stomach.

"Seriously I can't eat again for a week. I'm like one of those pythons that ingested a gazelle whole." Stella pointed at her ribs. "Look, you can see the antlers sticking out right here." She started laughing.

"Omigod. I saw a video like that one time on YouTube. I lost my appetite for a good hour after that."

"An hour?" Antoine cocked his head and grinned.

"What can I say? I'm a foodie. I mean it was disgusting but then again, sometimes what chefs do in a kitchen can be somewhat disgusting."

"What we do in our kitchen is far from disgusting," Domenico said.

"You work in a kitchen?" Stella said. It probably would have behooved her to have a slight inkling about what the man did professionally. Well, she knew about the whole family vineyard, but this kitchen gig was an intriguing turn of events.

"I run the events at Cantine dei Marchesi Romeo, and as part of that, I oversee the food prep for events. And more often than not, I roll up my sleeves and help out. I grew up cooking by my mamma's side, and I learned all the family recipes. It's that food that is served at events we host."

"Wow, so you actually are sort of one of us," Stella said.

"I don't know if I'd go that far, but I love food and fine wine and I love to make people happy with both. And I do so professionally. So I guess there are some similarities. I'm only lacking legitimate training."

"Does that bother you?" Stella said. She noticed that Alexa was totally engrossed in whatever loverboy was saying and in fact was practically sitting in his lap. You could get away with egregious public displays of affection a lot more easily in France it seemed.

Domenico shrugged. "I guess a little bit. I mean I don't know if it bothers me or if I'd enjoy having the foundation I've never had. Probably much of what I do has intuitively been what you do as a professional chef, but you know what I mean. Plus the idea of getting away, trying to expand my horizons a little became attractive to me. I needed to mix it up, get away for a while."

"*Sans déc*," Stella said. "I have an instructor who says that all the time. It means 'no kidding.' So does this mean you're staying in Paris?"

He shrugged. "For a while but not forever. I can only run away from home for so long. Once the weather cools we are going to have a lot more events at the vineyard and they'll need me for them. In the summer, we locals all leave and go to the sea, so there's no great demand for me. But soon, things will get crazy. For now I can manage my duties while here, but not for long."

Alexa interrupted their conversation and looked at the clock on her phone. "Um, if I'm not mistaken, Domenico, don't you have somewhere to go? With Stella?"

Stella knit her brows. "Uh, no."

Lexie wagged her finger at her. "*Mais non.* But no. You do in fact have someplace to go with none other than

Domenico Romeo. And I think you're going to love it. Now, off you go, Stella. *Ça roule ma poule.* Okay, chick, it's on." She gave her friend a pronounced wink as she stood up and dusted herself off and offered Antoine a hand up. "*A bientôt,* darlin'." *See you soon.*

Stella made a mental note never to trust Alexa again. Because she had no damned idea what her friend had gotten her into, but she was pretty sure it was something that she'd end up regretting. *Ça roule ma poule, my ass.*

Chapter Eighteen

DOMENICO could sense Stella tensing up the minute she knew she was going to be left on her own with him. Which did little for his self-esteem. Nothing like a woman bristling at being stuck with you to sort of kill the mood. But he remembered what he had planned and was confident she'd come around despite how prickly as she was.

He stood and offered his hand to her. They collected up her belongings and walked a short block to where a man in a white dinner jacket was waiting with a Lincoln Town car. He held the door for Stella and closed it once Domenico got in.

"Am I to presume I'm being kidnapped?" Stella said. "And if so, please tell me it doesn't involve handcuffs and blindfolds."

Domenico smiled. "You do expect the worst of me, don't you? Although I suppose handcuffs and blindfolds aren't always a bad thing." He grinned, knowing that would totally make her crazy. "Trust me, no bondage is on the menu."

The car drove for about ten minutes until it arrived at the ornately decorated Pont Alexander III, where they were led to a stunning mahogany Venetian water taxi.

"Now we're talking. You can't go wrong in an Italian boat in Paris." Domenico eyed the gleaming boat as he ushered Stella on board and the captain handed them each a glass of champagne.

"Why do I get the feeling this isn't going to be quite like the inexpensive champagne we had in our wine class?" Stella said.

Domenico nodded. "Well, I've taken it on as a personal challenge to persuade you that wines and champagnes can be exceptional. This is Krug Grand Cuvée. It's a step or two above what you've had before."

He tipped his glass to hers and she remembered what they'd been taught in class, so she held the glass up to the waning sunlight and carefully inspected the color. Next she swirled it gently and inhaled. Finally she pulled a sip into her mouth, allowing it to roll from front to back, exciting her taste buds, educating her mouth to the many layers of flavor in the wine.

She smiled. "You sure do know how to treat a woman. I don't know if I can ever go back to the cheap stuff."

"So you like?"

"I love," she said, sipping more as the captain began to explain the evening's plans.

They tucked into the private salon and sat down on the white leather banquette seats. The roof was opened up to the city as the lights went on. The boat pulled away from the slip and motored along the River Seine, first in the direction of the Eiffel Tower, illuminated so beautifully against the darkening sky.

"I've never seen *la tour Eiffel* from the water," Stella said as she stared at it. "It's magical, isn't it?"

"I've never actually been inside the Eiffel Tower."

Stella's eyes widened. "That's criminal! We'll need to do something about that. No self-respecting tourist can leave Paris without going to the top of the Eiffel Tower and drinking champagne."

Domenico was encouraged that she made it sound as if she would perhaps partake in such an adventure. With him. At the same time. "Ahhh… so you drank champagne there, did you?"

She shrugged. "I mean you sort of have to. And it was decent champagne. After all, this is France."

"I think I just might take you up on your offer if you're sure you can stand my company all the way up the elevators." A smile curved up one side of his face.

Stella seemed to ponder her answer for a moment. "How about we do things one step at a time." They stood and moved to the back of the boat onto a small well with two seats, but they both chose to sit on the top edge, admiring the Parisian skyline.

He nodded. "Fair enough. So talk to me about yourself some more. You, why you love to make cakes. What it's been like for you to live an ocean away from your previous life."

Stella sighed. "Let's see… Me and cooking…Where to begin?" she looked skyward as if that would provide the answer. "I once worked in a cupcake shop and it was there I realized everyone who came into the store left happy. To me, that was so telling, a testimonial to the transformative power of food. Even if you've had a lousy day, the simplest thing—a tiny cake—could make all the difference. I loved that.

"I decided to make that my goal—to make people happy with my food. Which I did to a certain degree with all the baking I did growing up, but then I truly focused on it. I'd bake dozens of cookies and drop them by a shelter in my town for battered women. I whipped up all sorts of confections for a rehab center for children with disabilities. I helped get a baking program started at a homeless haven, so that maybe some of those people could experience the small joys that came with creating something with your own hands."

Domenico remained silent and let her talk. The more he could reel her in, the better. Perhaps by sharing her stories, she might be comfortable enough to let her guard down. "So culinary school was the next step?"

"It took me awhile to save the money to come here. It's not cheap! But once I became immersed in pastry school, I fell in love with the cake end of things. After all, a beautiful wedding cake is sort of the pièce de résistance of the pastry world—at least to some. It makes me feel good to do my part although I'm super cynical about the ultimate outcome of those unions that were forged in lust and naïve optimism only to be forever marinated in a powerful dose of reality. Making wedding cakes is perfect for me because that's as close as I'll ever get to a wedding. I have no interest in staggering down that disastrous path."

Domenico stared at her, surprised at the vehemence of her feelings. "Wow. You don't hold the state of marriage in high esteem."

She shook her head. "No one's ever given me good reason for that. I had a deadbeat dad who took off with another woman, which was in itself a match made in hell. Had an alcoholic mother who lost herself in the bottle after my father deserted us and left me to fend for myself. And a wicked stepmother who would give Cinderella's a run for her money." She frowned, lost in thought momentarily. "Nope. No great reason ever presented to me for why I should think anything but that about marriage. Why? Do you think it's some brilliant invention?"

"Maybe I've got a smattering of hopeless romantic in me, but I do have great faith in marriage. My parents adored one another and were happily married for twenty-some years until my father died suddenly."

Stella thrust her lip in a pout. "Oh, Domenico. I'm so sorry."

He held his hands up "It's okay. It was awhile ago. But it was hard when it happened."

"How old were you?"

"I was a teenager. Not a good time to lose a father, to lose your role model. Our family took quite a hit when he passed. It shook us to our core, and everyone struggled to deal with the fallout from it." He looked away for a minute. He tried to not think about those days because they were so hard. No one needed to be reminded of pain in their lives.

"That's so tragic. I'm truly sorry for you."

"No worries. I wasn't looking for pity. We all have our crosses to bear in life. In many other ways, I've been nothing but terribly fortunate. I have a warm and loving family, a loving mother, a comfortable life."

"Lucky you. My comfortable life has started here, in this magical city."

"You've fallen in love with this city, haven't you?" he said, leaning over and kissing the tip of her nose.

"It's kind of hard not to."

He could relate to that. It was kind of hard not to fall for Stella Whitaker as well.

Chapter Nineteen

STELLA tried hard not to freeze. Here she was on a glamorous boat in the middle of the River Seine with this handsome, sexy, too-kind-for-words man she had developed feelings for, despite herself. She was so mad that she hadn't kept her guard up adequately to stop this from happening.

Yet while she lamented that, she was doing some serious soul-searching too. Here she was talking about how much she loved to bake because desserts and sweets made people happy. Yet she seemed incapable of putting out the least bit of effort to make Domenico happy, to return the favor. Because she could no longer deny that he was doing his damnedest to please her in every way, shape, and form.

Why could she not simply climb out of that skin she had insisted on wearing, like those protective stinger suits they wear to surf in Australia so they don't get stung by deadly jellyfish? She didn't have to safeguard herself like she did. She'd become so habituated to doing so. But she was starting to think she'd outgrown that skin—it was tight and uncomfortable and confining. Maybe it was time for her to live a little and stop being afraid.

Domenico was playing with her hair, twirling it in his fingers as if running fine sand between them. But he said nothing, leaving this pregnant silence looming over them. She didn't know where to begin to say what she wanted to say. She wasn't sure if she could say it.

"You know, Domenico." She took a deep breath. "I'm sorry for writing that mean stuff about you on the airplane. For that matter, I'm sorry I was such a bitch to you at the airport. Well, both airports. Well, sort of it's been an ongoing theme, hasn't it?"

He brought his finger to her lips to stop her. "Shhh," he said. "No need to apologize."

"But there is," she said. "I've been quite rude, and I feel bad about it."

He started to laugh. "When I read that message you wrote on the plane, I thought it was hilarious. And ballsy. I loved that about it. You didn't hold back. Which is what I think made me fall for you. You clearly had a lot of passion."

"Yeah, but it was angry passion."

"It's okay, often passion can take many forms. But it showed that you have strong feelings, that you can care. Although I must admit I was pretty surprised how quickly it switched from one side to another with you. By morning you wanted to kill me, and by the light of the moon you were ready to make love with me." He reached for her hands and twined his fingers with hers.

Stella flinched at that phrase. Make love. Is that what they did? Wasn't it simply good old sex? *Make love* sounded so committal, so intentional, more than a blurred frenzy beneath the sheets.

"To be truthful, I just wanted to scratch that itch, you know?"

Domenico frowned. "Great. So does that make me the flea? Or the dog? Either way, I'm flattered." His smile was wistful.

Stella squeezed his hand. "It makes you the brave man who was willing to put yourself out there for someone who wasn't particularly capable of reciprocating."

He laughed a little. "Do you know how many times I've reread those notes you wrote?"

"What do you mean, reread them? I thought they'd disappeared into the ether. At least I had hoped as much."

He shrugged. "Sorry, but I took pictures of the screen with my phone. I hope that doesn't sound too stalkerish. But the thing is, it turned me on when I realized you thought I was sexy and were thinking about my cock. I couldn't think of anything but getting you naked from that point on."

"Wait a second—you read those notes and got turned on?"

He nodded as if stating the obvious. "Of course. I'm a guy. A girl mentions how big your cock is, and that's a turn-on."

"But I was being a jerk about it."

"It doesn't matter. Between the lines: you wanted my cock."

She swatted at him. "That's a little, uh, cocky." She smiled.

"Don't get me wrong. You put up enough roadblocks to stop any guy from getting too hot and bothered. Enough that if it weren't for your persistent friend, I'd have probably thrown in the towel."

"You mean my interventionist roommate?"

"Your thoughtful roommate who wanted to help you."

"Help me get laid?"

"Maybe. But help you get past whatever trauma has been holding you back."

"But what if it's something I can't let go of."

"Look, Stella, you were brave enough to drop everything and cross an ocean to carve out a life for yourself other than what you seemed fated to. I'd say that's evidence enough that you're able to let things go."

"Can we take this slow and see? I'm not sure if I trust myself."

"We can go as slow as you'd like. As long as you don't cut me off. Now that I've had a chance to be with you, I can't take that." His finger was toying with the thin strap of her camisole top, gradually tugging it down. He pulled her toward him and pressed his lips to hers as his fingers tugged down the strap and slipped beneath the top to toy with her breasts.

Stella opened her mouth to him and their tongues stroked and tangled and danced with one another, their breathing increasing as his hand massaged her breasts, and his other hand reached down to unbutton her shorts, then slip beneath the top edge of her panties.

"Domenico, the boat captain—"

He shushed her with his mouth, his tongue tracing her lips and finding her mouth again, where he slicked his tongue along her teeth, her gums, her own hungry tongue. "It's pitch dark out. The captain can't see us all the way back here. Besides, he's steering the boat. His back is to us."

Stella was still conflicted. Most of her wanted nothing more than to shrug off her fears and yield to Domenico. His touch did crazy things to her. She could barely contain her thoughts against the sensation of his warm fingers stroking along her lips, already so wet from his ministrations. They slid inside of her and pressed, deep, first one finger, then two, then three. She was mad with the sensations racing through her belly and down to her pelvis. But every now and then the practical Stella reared its uptight head, reminding her that she didn't "do" relationships. That men left. That nothing good could come of this. But then Domenico's mouth was on her nipple, sucking, hard, and his teeth nipped her and his fingers pumped harder and harder against her wet center. And she could shut up practical Stella long enough as her muscles coiled low in her belly, and her body erupted in pleasure. Her center clenched down on Domenico's fingers as his tongue toyed with her breast. She pressed her hips hard against him, and he held her tightly as she rode out her climax.

They remained like that for a few heartbeats as Stella's breathing calmed down. Domenico slid his hands from beneath her panties, bringing his fingers to his mouth and licking them each, slowly, deliberately, before he settled his lips over hers and kissed her hard.

Which was when, as usual, the panic set in.

"Domenico," she said, trying to figure out the best way to say this. "I love when you do that to me but it's not fair to you. I mean really, this can't go anywhere. I know we can have some fun together, but you and me…"

Domenico pulled back and perched on the edge of the seat with his legs spread, his elbows resting on his knees, his head in his hands.

He scrubbed his fingers through his hair, about to speak, when the boat suddenly swerved, and Domenico went flying, right off the side of the boat into the dark waters of the Seine.

Chapter Twenty

"DOMENICO!" Stella yelled, waving her arms as she ran to the front of the boat. *"Capitaine! Il est dans la rivière!"*

She pulled on the captain's shoulder and pointed desperately toward the spot where he flew off the boat. "You need to hurry!"

The water was dark and there was the danger of another boat hitting him. Despite the late hour, there were still Bateaux Mouches cruising along the Seine as well as smaller craft like the one they were in.

She kept jumping up and down, pointing toward where she thought she saw him bobbing in the water. It was so hard to see in the dark. She was terrified. It was all her fault. Here he was, again, being so sweet, so thoughtful, worried only about her pleasure, trying to show her how he felt about her, and she lost it again. Such. Complete. Chickenshit.

"Monsieur," she said. *"Se dépêcher!"* Hurry!

The boat looped back and circled several times when over the din of the motor Stella could hear Domenico calling her name.

"That way," she said, pointing for the captain. "Go slowly so you don't run him over!"

The boat chugged along and finally, she saw one arm waving to her.

"Stella! Here!"

She finally spotted him and helped to guide the captain to where he was, and she tossed a life preserver overboard, then pulled the rope back. She lowered the step ladder at the back of the boat and Domenico climbed aboard, grasping Stella's arm for balance.

She pulled him toward her and wrapped her arms around him. "Oh, Domenico, look at you." She stretched her arms to get a good look while holding on to him still. "You're drenched. You must be freezing."

He wiped the water from his face. "It's not so bad. If this had happened in January, I'd have been in more trouble."

"But you could have died!"

"More like died of embarrassment."

"There's nothing to be embarrassed about."

"Oh, except for yet again, for all of my desperate efforts with you, I got shut down. I guess that was the ultimate cold shower, being flung overboard like that."

Stella frowned. "I'm sorry—"

He held up his hands. "It's fine, Stella. I get it. You're not that into me. Now let's get this captain to take us back to shore and we can go our separate ways. No hard feelings."

"But—"

"I think we both realize it's for the better. You don't need some man nagging you, and my ego doesn't need the rejection. Besides, I have things to focus on while I'm here, so perhaps the distraction would have been an unnecessary one anyhow."

Stella sighed. This wasn't how she wanted to end things. She felt horrible. And confused. And conflicted. And annoyed. And wrong. Because after she shed all of those other emotions and her own self-preservation concerns, she knew ultimately she was making a terrible, terrible decision. But she had no idea how to rectify it.

Stella was left to fester on her own once she returned to the apartment, still wet from hugging Domenico. It seemed Alexa had left the apartment alone just in case... Just in case Stella had remembered to not be a heartless jerk. Just in case Stella had decided to not be a coward. Just in case Stella had decided to toss her heart into the ring and take a chance.

She finally lay down in her bed and cried. Cried for the little girl who was so broken that she couldn't allow herself to be happy when happiness was pounding on her door. More like clubbing her over the head with it.

When she could cry no more, she drifted off to a restless sleep, and by dawn, she only felt worse about everything. What a schmuck she was. But Domenico had made it clear, he'd had enough. She needed to respect his wishes.

It didn't get any easier when Alexa showed up around lunchtime, excited to hear about her night.

"Don't ask," Stella said. Her tearstained face was a dead giveaway that things hadn't unfolded quite as expected.

"Awww, Stel, what now?"

Stella proceeded to tell her the story, ending with a world-weary sigh, her shoulders sagging beneath the weight of her failure.

"So how does this make you feel, honey?" Alexa asked.

"Really shitty."

Alexa lifted an eyebrow. "Good!"

"Good?"

"Yes, of course. Great, in fact."

"How so?"

"Because a) that means your little heart hurts. Which means your little heart is capable of feeling love. Which is a great thing. And b) because that means you're ready to fix this."

Stella started to cry. "But it's not fixable. I blew it."

Alexa waved at her as if shooing away an annoying fly. "Don't be silly. These things can always be fixed." She handed her roomie a tissue. "Now wipe your eyes. We've got some scheming to do."

Chapter Twenty-One

"I appreciate your reaching out to me, Alexa," Domenico said. "I know you meant well trying to facilitate me and Stella getting together. I'm afraid it wasn't meant to be."

They were walking out of the Champ de Mars metro stop, en route to the Eiffel Tower.

"I'm sorry I kept leading you on like that. I honestly thought maybe she could do it. I guess she's not quite ready to let her heart go. I don't understand it—if I was single I'd go for you in a heartbeat—but I guess it's hard to get past the past. I'm glad you were willing to come out tonight. I pictured you alone in your hotel room and I knew that was crazy. Plus you've never been to the Eiffel Tower. We'll meet Antoine there—he's picking up the tickets. It's the least I can do."

"Really, you did not have to do that."

"But I want to."

He shrugged. "Fine. I'm yours for the evening."

They met up with Antoine, who was waiting with their tickets at the West Pillar. The three of them got in line and waited for the elevator to go up, piling in with the crush of tourists who were also hoping to see the twinkling lights of Paris from high atop the tower. They boarded the second elevator that took them to the top and walked out to a breathtaking view of Paris.

"Come, let's go grab a glass of champagne. As we've said, you have to have champagne at the top of the Eiffel Tower."

Domenico was thinking about the last time he'd had champagne. Had that been twenty-four hours? It seemed like a lifetime ago in some odd way.

He followed Alexa and Antoine and when they arrived at the tiny bar, Stella stepped out of the shadow, two glasses of rosé champagne in her hands.

"I think I can take it from here, Lex," she said, giving her friend a hug.

"He's all yours. And do me a favor: don't blow it. My heart can't take this drama anymore."

Stella rolled her eyes. "Tell me about it."

Alexa and Antoine waved good-bye to the two of them and walked off in the dark, to the far side of the tower, leaving Stella and Domenico in peace.

Stella reached for Domenico's hand and guided him to an open spot along the railing, overlooking the breathtaking city below. "It was pretty cowardly of me to let you go last night," she said.

"But—"

"Hush." She held a finger to his lips. "It's my turn." She leaned over and pressed her lips to his for a second. "I know I've got some issues. I'm trying to figure things out. But the last thing I want to do is drive you away. Domenico—"

"Honestly, Stella, you don't have to say this."

"Oh, but I do." She lifted her champagne glass to his and tipped it against it. "Because, see, Domenico, somehow you managed to slip beneath my defenses. I don't know how you did it. You got past the moat. And the crocodiles and the soldiers shooting poison-tipped arrows and the other ones pouring boiling oil from the ramparts. I have this whole army surrounding my fortress, all set up to protect me from loving anyone. But I realized now that it's probably the stupidest thing in the world to deny myself love. So I'm going to stop being the chickenshit little girl who ran away from feelings and instead I'm going to open myself up to you and share them." She took a deep breath and a swig of champagne for fortification. "Domenico Romeo, I'm afraid that I'm falling in love with you. And I understand if you're completely sick of my nonsense and want nothing to do with me ever again, but if you could find it in your heart to forgive me, well, I promise you, I'm going to try hard to honor you by not pulling the stupid shenanigans I've been pulling on you. I'm going to open up my heart to you. I only ask that you're gentle with it."

Domenico smiled. "That's a lot of burden on my shoulders, caring for a fragile heart." He pulled her toward him with his finger on her chin. "And I'm honored to be the man to carry that responsibility. I promise you won't be disappointed. But there's one thing."

Stella frowned. "I'm afraid to ask what."

He broke into a broad smile. "If you can please promise to keep me away from dangerous boat captains on the Seine?"

She pulled him toward her by the collar, kissing him hard. "It's a fair trade: my heart for your safety."

"And maybe one other thing?"

She lifted her brow.

"You still owe me a cake."

"As long as it doesn't have to be a wedding cake."

He smiled. "Not yet. Not quite yet. But never say never."

They clinked champagne flutes—because, after all, she was now a fan of good champagne, and she leaned over and kissed him. "Never again will I say never to love."

Thank you so much for reading *Blue-Blooded Romeo!* I hope you enjoyed it! If so, please help others find this book:

1. Help other people find this book by writing a review.

2. Sign up for my new releases email so you can find out about the next book as soon as it's available and get fun giveaways.
   http://eepurl.com/baaewn

3. Like my Facebook page.
   www.facebook.com/jennygardinerbooks

And I love to hear from readers! Let me know what you think about my books! You can write to me at jenny@jennygardiner.net, and visit me on the web at www.jennygardiner.net.

Turn the page for a sneak peek of the next book in The Royal Romeos – **Big O Romeo.**

Big O Romeo

Chapter One

IF there was one thing Francesco Romeo hated more than having to attend a party full of strangers, it was having to attend a *costume* party full of strangers dressed in stupid outfits. So it was with great reluctance that he agreed to attend the 70th birthday party of his mother's best friend, Elettra Giovanetti, who'd decreed that their little corner of Tuscany hadn't had a decent costume party in what seemed like centuries. In Francesco's humble opinion, it hadn't been long enough. Because to him, there was no such thing as a decent costume party.

For one thing, people tended to dress like fools at those things. Men usually looked like complete imbeciles, and women often felt the need to indulge in their inner beer wench, which, okay, sometimes wasn't such a bad thing—at least from a visual perspective—but seriously, it was just downright odd when women took on the persona of the outfit they had on.

He still remembered the last such party he'd attended, when a voluptuously-shaped lady who had been a teacher of his in primary school donned a cleavage-revealing corset-top, wedged a cup of maraschino cherries between her generous bosom, and insisted that guests pop her cherry all night long. You just couldn't un-see that shit.

Particularly when it belonged to the woman who taught you the alphabet, phonics, and how to get along with others.

And for another thing, it's just weird, standing there talking to your hairdresser, who's pretending to be Dorothy from the Wizard of Oz, when all along you know she's just Maria Valdetti with the distinctive mole on the tip of her nose, who's been styling your hair since you were about fourteen years old. The whole thing seemed sadly regressive to him.

Nevertheless he found himself at the party rental shop minutes before closing time, waiting in line for a Three Musketeers costume, at the behest of his mother, who he hated to displease. It didn't matter that there weren't two other musketeers to complete the theme. Neither his brothers nor friends would agree to wear hats with feathers—they were for sissies, they claimed—plus all the more normal costumes had been rented by the time Francesco finally sucked it up and went in search of something to wear to this miserable party.

He was seriously regretting not snatching up the Darth Vader costume before it was nabbed by a wiser party-goer. At the time he figured it would impede his chances to make out with a woman, what with his entire face being covered by a mask. In hindsight perhaps that would have been a better alternative.

Because his remaining choices were to go as a 17th-century French swashbuckler, or settle for the oversized, body odor-drenched Barney the Purple Dinosaur costume, which he was certain hadn't been either cleaned or worn in about twenty years. At least he had a chance of getting laid in his chosen costume. Though between the girlie stockings, thigh-high leather boots, and, yeah, that gargantuan damned feather that kept obscuring his vision, he wasn't banking on much of any action from anyone under the age of three hundred.

He'd waited till, quite literally, the last possible minute to grab his threads, which meant he'd have to change clothes at the shop, which probably wasn't such a bad thing, since it spared him the ridicule at home. Though naturally his brothers would double-down on it once they found him at the party. He hoped that in the thick of the crowd they'd miss finding him. Besides, he was going to be cloaked in so much frippery maybe he'd go unnoticed altogether. A man could only hope.

Allie Ledbetter was nervous about this party. New to the area and not particularly fluent in Italian, she wasn't sure if it was a good thing or a bad thing that she was going to be basically invisible at the costume party she was invited to attend in honor of the mother of her new boss, Giovanni Giovanetti. Apparently he was throwing the fête for her seventieth birthday. It felt a little weird showing up at a stranger's party for such an auspicious occasion. But oh, well. In her line of work she had become accustomed to integrating into whatever environment she found herself in temporarily, even if it meant showing up at some granny's birthday shindig.

Besides, Allie loved a good costume party; it was fun to see how very creative people could get for them. In fact back home, she'd dressed in many elaborate get-ups for Halloween parties over the years, once even donning a multi-layered, hoop-skirted Marie Antoinette costume. But far from home and minus her trusty sewing machine, she was going to have to make do with a more rudimentary outfit, but one that always seemed to work for last-minute.

On a day-trip to Rome she'd found some perfect crushed black velvet at *Fratelli Bassetti Tessuti*, a renowned fabric shop favored by the country's fashion cognoscenti. She picked up some sewing notions including a packet of needles, straight pins, black thread and fabric scissors, and even found some fiberfill. Back in Tuscany, she sat on the terrace of the plush guest cottage of Giovanetti Vineyards sipping Chianti as the intense summer sun hung low in the sky, having a thoroughly lovely time hand-stitching and stuffing her cat tail and securing kitty cat ears onto a headband as well. Her costume came together with a black satin camisole top and a pair of black skinny jeans. With her long, wavy streaky blonde hair and hazel eyes, she'd make a perfectly acceptable feline for the night.

When the time came to dress for the party, Allie drew thick, black Cleopatra-style eyeliner along the edge of her lids, slicked on some extra layers of mascara, and wrapped her tresses along the fat wand of her curling iron to create cascading curls. She debated going all-in with whiskers and decided it was necessary to complete the transformation, so traced slender whisker lines along her cheeks, then finished the look by coloring the tip of her nose black with an eyebrow pencil.

She pinned the tail to her jeans and tugged them on, then slipped on the delicate cami top. She stood sideways, looking at herself in the full-length mirror, pressed her hands along her thighs to straighten out her jeans, and gave a nod.

"Not too bad," she said as she reached for a pair of strappy black sandals to complete the look. She slid on the headband ears, and slipped out the door of the cottage.

She walked along a slate pathway to the main house, a sprawling pale pink two-story stucco *palazzo* like the many that peppered the hillsides in this part of Tuscany. Expensive cars lined the driveway and a throng of guests paraded through the rose garden as they made their way to the dramatic front entryway of the Giovanetti home. She'd only been in Tuscany for a few days, but so far what she'd seen sure made her want to stay. Between the rolling hillsides clad in patchworked fields with rows of vines now heavy with fruit, or cloaked with the gnarled branches of ancient olive trees, this land felt magical. Throw in magnificent manor homes that had witnessed history over many hundreds of years, the late-day color of light that was some breathtaking combination of damask rose and ripe melon, and, well, there was something about this place that spoke to her.

She entered through the massive oak doors that were drawn open on this temperate summer evening and was handed a flute of top-tier Italian Prosecco and escorted by a waiter dressed like one of Cinderella's footmen to a wide, dramatic tiled terrace along the back of the palazzo that overlooked the valley below. High above, a flock of starlings darted to and fro and she felt a momentary pang of anxiety, knowing that in a matter of days it was going to be her job—well, hers and Lola's, her trusty peregrine falcon—to ensure those starlings stayed clear of her bosses' grapes. It's what she'd been doing for a couple of years now, first in California, letting Lola and other birds of prey loose to intimidate the population of birds that constantly vex the growers of wine grapes.

Lola had become well-known after Allie had given a series of lectures about this at several wine-growers conventions, and Giovanni had reached out to her shortly thereafter in the hopes of bringing her to Tuscany to attempt to minimize the frustrating and at times astronomical loss of grapes leading up to his grape harvest thanks to greedy starlings. Thoughts of Lola would wait till the morning, because tonight she was given a free pass to not worry about her charge and instead enjoy herself.

She marveled at the creativity of some of the costumes she saw people wearing. One woman dressed as Little Red Riding Hood clutched a leash attached to a gorgeous white and gray huskie dog with bright blue eyes wearing a sleeping cap and purple pajamas: the Big Bad Wolf doing business as Grandma. Very clever.

A man moseyed by dressed as a stick figure, wearing an all-white outfit on which the black stick shape had been painted. There was a couple in which the woman dressed as a mermaid and the man, a fierce Father Neptune. Another person was dressed as an octopus. There was a hula dancer and a Barbie look-alike, and several zombies, though she couldn't help but think it wouldn't be particularly fun to get up close and personal with a man oozing faux bodily fluids. Yep, zombie was not the costume to wear if you went to the party in search of a love interest.

Not that she was on the prowl or anything: for one thing she wasn't going to be staying here for long. Once the grapes were harvested, she would move on to another gig. Plus, after her last fiasco of a relationship in which her fiancé Ben decided it made sense to let her know only weeks before the wedding that he actually preferred men, she was a little gun-shy over guys. So tonight, she was going to just have her look, enjoy some drinks, perhaps make some small talk if anyone spoke enough English to conduct a conversation with, and then call it a night. Or so she thought.

"Meow." She heard a deep, resonant voice purr behind her. She turned to see the perhaps the most handsome man she'd ever laid eyes on, with sooty, soulful brown eyes and wavy, rich, peat-colored hair that just about begged for her fingers to run through. He was dressed as one of the Three Musketeers, which just so happened to top Allie's fantasy of the type of man she'd love to be taken by. It fit with her love of falconry and her passion for the romance of the adventurous days of swashbuckling men clinking swords and defending fair maidens.

Damn. This particular musketeer could defend her honor any damned day.

She let out a purr of contentment.

So much for avoiding men for a while.

Chapter Two

FRANCESCO decided he had to dial down his disdain for costume parties. Sure the woman standing by the bar dressed as Elvira, Mistress of the Night did not appeal to him, despite her voluminous breasts that were more than peaking out of the cleavage-baring V in her dress that went all the way to her navel. There was something to be said for leaving a little bit to the imagination.

And the buxom woman dressed as a milkmaid who asked if he wanted to squeeze her teats was just a little too obvious. Maybe if he was feeling super desperate... but no. Not even then.

But then he laid eyes on the kitty cat standing alone against the limestone balustrade on the terrace and he decided he needed to re-evaluate his blanket revulsion of this particular party genre. Because wow, meow, that one instantly took his breath away. He'd love to stroke that kitty cat, in more ways than one.

The tail alone... And by tail—while his curiosity was certainly piqued by the velvety one dangling from her butt—what he really meant was that ass, perfectly shapely in a pair of tight jeans that hugged those two round globes, one of his many favorite parts of a woman. As an added bonus, her legs went on and on, ending in some sexy little high-heeled sandals, complete with vampy black polish on her toes. His eyes scanned up her body and stopped at nipples that were poking out from her silky top, leaving him curious—make that desperate—to see even more. As his gaze continued upward, he was especially pleased with her face: bowed lips in an innocent smile and wide, kind, earthy-golden eyes that fit her cat costume perfectly, topped by coils of shiny, blonde waves he'd love to grab onto while she... he had to tamp down that thought or he'd scare the poor kitty away.

Meow indeed.

He decided he had nothing to lose—after all, he was dressed like a damned musketeer—so he snuck up behind her and purred into her ear.

She turned around and just stared. He wasn't sure if it was the crazy get-up he was wearing or what that caused her to not say a word, and it made him nervous to think he looked like a giant wanker and she was just devising how many different ways to tell him to beat it.

But she then lifted a brow and smiled. "Well, hi there, stranger." She made a point of looking him up and down. "I gotta say, I love a man in tights."

And Francesco breathed a sigh of relief because there were likely far more women turned off by that than on.

"Then that makes us even because I love a beautiful pussy when I see one."

She laughed. "I'm not sure whether to laugh or be shocked at your impertinence."

"Impertinence? Me?" he batted his eyelashes in jest.

"I was trying to use a word that a damsel in distress in the time of the musketeers might use."

"You tend to mine the language of antiquity?"

She shook her head. "Nah. I've just read plenty of historical romance novels."

Francesco cocked his head. "You mean bodice rippers?"

Allie scrunched her nose. "No one uses that term any more. After all, I'm not reading novels where rogue men force themselves on women."

"What do these rogue men do, then?"

She laughed. "Sorry, this is sort of a weird conversation. I guess I'd say they seduce their way in. Much kinder and gentler that way."

"So it's the seduction that appeals to you."

Allie lifted a curious brow. "Doesn't that appeal to pretty much everyone?"

He held his hands up. "You'll find no argument with me. I'm a big fan of the seduction."

She sized him up again. "With an outfit like that, you'll hardly have to lift a finger."

"Ahhh, so then all I need to do is discuss the size of my… peacock feather to win the hand of a fair maiden?" He flicked the thing hanging over his eyes and smiled broadly.

She blurted out a laugh. "Well, I know I always love a man with a big… feather." She fingered the large one dangling in front of his face. "Though I suspect this is an ostrich feather and has absolutely nothing to do with a cock, pea- or larger."

Francesco's interest was indeed piqued. This woman was surprisingly comfortable making suggestive conversation with the likes of him. How could he not want to see where this led?

He held out his hand. "Francesco Romeo," he said, reaching for hers.

Allie extended her hand and he gently pulled it toward his lips and pressed them to the back of her fingers. She blushed, which he loved, as it showed him that while she was not afraid to get sassy with him, she also had some moral constraints that probably gave her great internal conflict. Clearly it wasn't the norm for her to talk to a man like this. Maybe it was the costume—it let her hide behind it to reveal a more unencumbered version of herself. He'd take this over the cherry-popping beer wench any day.

"I'm Allie. Allie Ledbetter."

"Enchanted. Or as we say in Italy, *incantato*."

"Incantato…" she played with the word on her tongue, which made him want to reach out with his own tongue and tangle their words together. "In France it would be *enchanté. N'est-ce pas*?"

"You speak French?"

She shrugged and held up her hand with a small space between thumb and forefinger. "*Un peu.* A little bit."

"*Parlo Italiano*?"

She shook her head. "I've tried to learn a little with the Duo Lingo app, but I'd embarrass myself if I attempted to communicate with it. But by all means, please do use your mother tongue. It makes me swoon just a bit to listen to Italian being spoken."

Francesco rubbed his hands together. "So I've got three things in my favor: I'm dressed like a swashbuckling man of yore, which turns you on. I speak Italian, which makes you swoon. And of course there's that big, uh, feather of mine. What more do I need to convince you of my worth and honor?"

"Yikes," she said, wagging her finger. "I suppose I showed my hand too soon. Remind me next time to keep my big mouth shut."

"*A il contrario.*" He rubbed his stubbled chin with his thumb and forefinger. "To the contrary. For me it's quite a turn-on when a woman owns her sexuality."

She blushed again. Even the pale skin on her chest turned rosy. He wondered if the soft flesh just beneath the edge of her shirt had also shaded pink. He imagined slipping his fingers beneath the edge of the silky black fabric and his mouth grew dry. Clearly it had been too long since he'd been laid.

"Speaking of size," she said, reaching for the cutlass secured to his waistband. "I like your saber."

"Why, thank you. And it's sized to your satisfaction?" He knew he might be pushing the envelope with his double entrendres, but he decided to go for broke.

"The bigger the better." She licked her lips. "But I wonder—"

Francesco couldn't wait to hear what she wondered. He hoped it had something to do with the many uses of that oversized épée of his.

"Why do musketeers carry swords—aren't they supposed to be all about the musket?"

So much for a suggestive innuendo. But he had a rebound response to get back on track. "Because swords are far sexier."

"Oh really?" she crossed her arms over her chest. "How so?"

"You can use your imagination." He drew his sword. "Imagining where that sword might penetrate." He lifted the sabre and gently drew it beneath her breasts, like a threatening Barbary Coast pirate might. "Isn't this how they do it? Here," He said, moving the small, rounded tip and pressing it toward her pubic bone. "Or here?"

"Hmmm," she said. "I would think if you were looking for penetration with something that size you'd have some other more appealing options."

His eyes grew wide. Then they were interrupted by a very drunk man dressed as a monkey asking where the bar was.

Francesco turned to Allie and reached his arm out to link with hers. "What say we tuck into a more private corner where we could at least monkey around without being interrupted by strange simians?"

They walked toward the furthest end of the terrace, far from the crowd, where there were no lights and they could have some privacy.

"You're not quite like any woman I've met before," he said.

She shrugged. "I'm just plain old me."

He shook his head. "Trust me, there is nothing plain about you. I know a gorgeous pussy when I see one."

She blushed again and playfully smacked her hand to his chest. "Stop. You're embarrassing me."

"Mea culpa," he said. "I don't want to make you feel uncomfortable." He pointed to the far corner of the stone railing. "I have something I want to show you."

He steered her up against the railing and stood behind her, pointing far off to the right. "Can you see it?"

She turned her head in the direction he was pointing. "What?"

"There," he said, nodding in that direction. "The full moon is just beginning to rise on the horizon. You can barely see an orange sliver as it creeps skyward."

"Ahhh," she said. "It's beautiful."

"It's known as the thunder moon," he said. "Because of the propensity for volatile storms at this time of year."

"Sounds tempestuous."

"Lively and heated. Just the way I like it." Francesco came up behind Allie, leaning his body against her back and bringing his arms around her, tucking his thumbs into the front pockets of her jeans. He could feel himself growing larger as he pressed along that sweet kitty-cat tail of hers.

"I thought you'd sheathed that saber of yours." She turned and gave him a sly look with a wink.

He leaned down and nibbled on the edge of her ear as he whispered into it. "Sometimes it just doesn't want to be so confined."

She pressed her ass up against him and he moaned. His mouth trailed along her ear, delivering tiny kisses and bites, then along her jawline until his lips found hers and he paused, pressing his lips to hers. Allie turned her head slightly and opened her mouth to him, allowing him to slick his tongue along the edge of her teeth as he sought out her tongue. She moaned and slid hers along his, deepening the kiss.

Francesco slid his hands along Allie's hips, moving up toward her breasts, where he cupped his hands over each one, rubbing them as she reached behind to press his body toward her even more, which thrust her breasts toward his reach. Francesco took that as a sign and moved his fingers along the top edge of her camisole, sliding his fingers down, nudging her barely-there strapless bra out of the way as his fingers sought those hard nipples he'd so wanted to feel earlier. He pressed them between his thumb and forefinger, massaging them as he felt them grow tighter in his fingers. She gasped. Good lord, if he wasn't careful he was going to lose it right here on the terrace of his mother's best friend's palazzo, which would so not be cool. He broke the kiss but continued to play with her nipples and massage her breasts.

"How about we slip away from here and maybe go catting around the neighborhood for a while. If you're lucky maybe I'll even howl at the moon like a good Tomcat." Francesco practically hummed the words in her ear.

Allie bit her lip as if contemplating her options. "This is all happening so fast," she said. "I mean on the one hand, yeesh. I've never made out with a musketeer before, so I'd love to keep playing. But on the other hand, we've barely introduced ourselves to one another. It's probably a good idea to put the brakes on this for the time being."

Francesco's lip thrust out in a pout. "But we were having so much fun." He shifted around so that they were face-to-face.

Allie squinted. "I know. I'm sorry. I just let myself get carried away. It must have been the costume. I let my guard down. I've really got to focus on my work. I can't allow distractions like this to get in the way."

"Distraction?" He frowned. "Here I thought we had a mutual attraction."

She shrugged. "Attraction. Distraction. I don't know. But I need to run. It was fun, though."

With that she turned and ran off toward the exit, not even turning to say goodbye.

"But I didn't even get your number," Francesco said, but she was too far away to even hear him. He scrubbed his hand over his face and looked down to his palm, which was smeared with black make-up that had transferred from Allie's face to his. All that was left of the best time he'd had in a long time.

Dammit, he hated costume parties.

Big O Romeo

coming September 26, 2017.

About the Author

Jenny Gardiner is the author of #1 Kindle Bestseller *Slim to None* and the award-winning novel *Sleeping with Ward Cleaver*. Her latest works are the *It's Reigning Men* series, featuring *Something in the Heir*, *Heir Today Gone Tomorrow*, *Bad to the Throne; Love is in the Heir*, *Shame of Thrones*; *Throne for a Loop; It's Getting Hot in Heir; A Court Gesture;* and her new Royal Romeos series, featuring *Red-Hot Romeo; Black Sheep Romeo*, *Red Carpet Romeo*, *Blue Collar Romeo*, *Silver Spoon Romeo*, *Blue-Blooded Romeo*, and the upcoming *Big O Romeo*. She also published the memoir *Winging It: A Memoir of Caring for a Vengeful Parrot Who's Determined to Kill Me,* now re-titled *Bite Me: a Parrot, a Family and a Whole Lot of Flesh Wounds*; the novels *Anywhere but Here*; *Where the Heart Is*; the essay collection *Naked Man on Main Street*, and *Accidentally on Purpose* and *Compromising Positions* (writing as Erin Delany); and is a contributor to the humorous dog anthology *I'm Not the Biggest Bitch in This Relationship*.

Her work has been found in Ladies Home Journal, the Washington Post, Marie-Claire.com, and on NPR's Day to Day. She was also a columnist for Charlottesville's Daily Progress for over a decade, and is the Volunteer Coordinator for the Virginia Film Festival.

She has worked as a professional photographer, an orthodontic assistant (learning quite readily that she was not cut out for a career in polyester), a waitress (probably her highest-paying job), a TV reporter, a pre-obituary writer, as well as a publicist to a United States Senator (where she first learned to write fiction). She's photographed Prince Charles (and her assistant husband got him to chuckle!), Elizabeth Taylor, and the president of Uganda. She and her family and menagerie of pets now live a less exotic life in Virginia.

Visit Jenny at her website at www.jennygardiner.net where you can sign up for her newsletter, visit her blog, or find her on Facebook and Twitter. And every blue moon she'll post adorable pictures of her pets on Instagram as @thejennygardiner.